ORPHAN'S QUEST

VOLUME 1

THE GREAT FORGET FANTASY SERIES

TERRY IRONWOOD

All rights reserved. No part of this publication may be reproduced, stored or transmitted in any form or by any means, electronic, mechanical, photocopying, recording, scanning, or otherwise without written permission from the publisher. It is illegal to copy this book, post it to a website, or distribute it by any other means without permission.

Copyright © 2024 by Terry Ironwood

This novel is entirely a work of fiction. The names, characters and incidents portrayed in it are the work of the author's imagination. Any resemblance to actual persons, living or dead, events or localities is entirely coincidental.

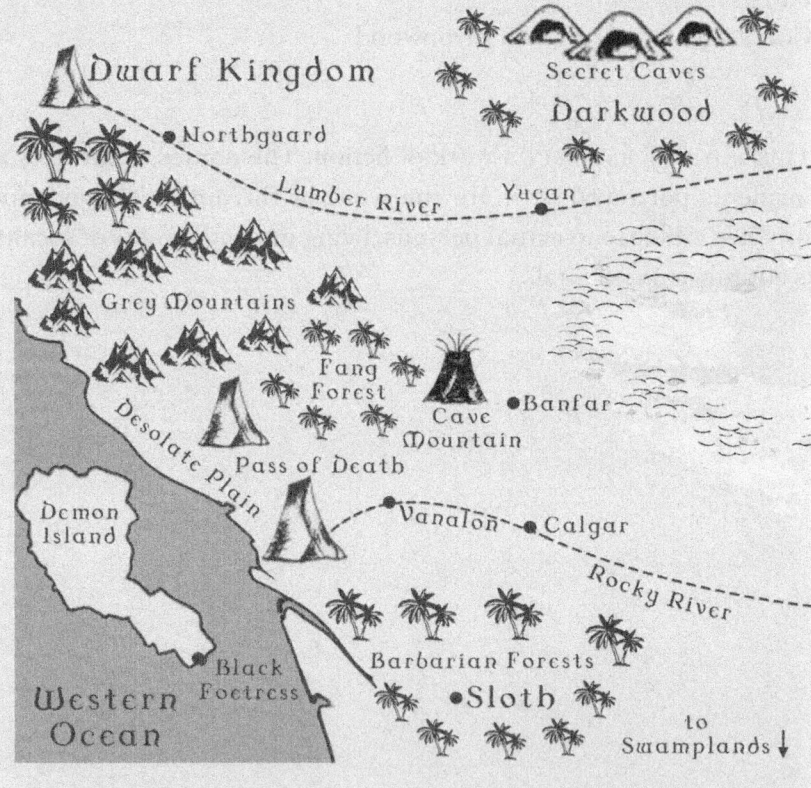

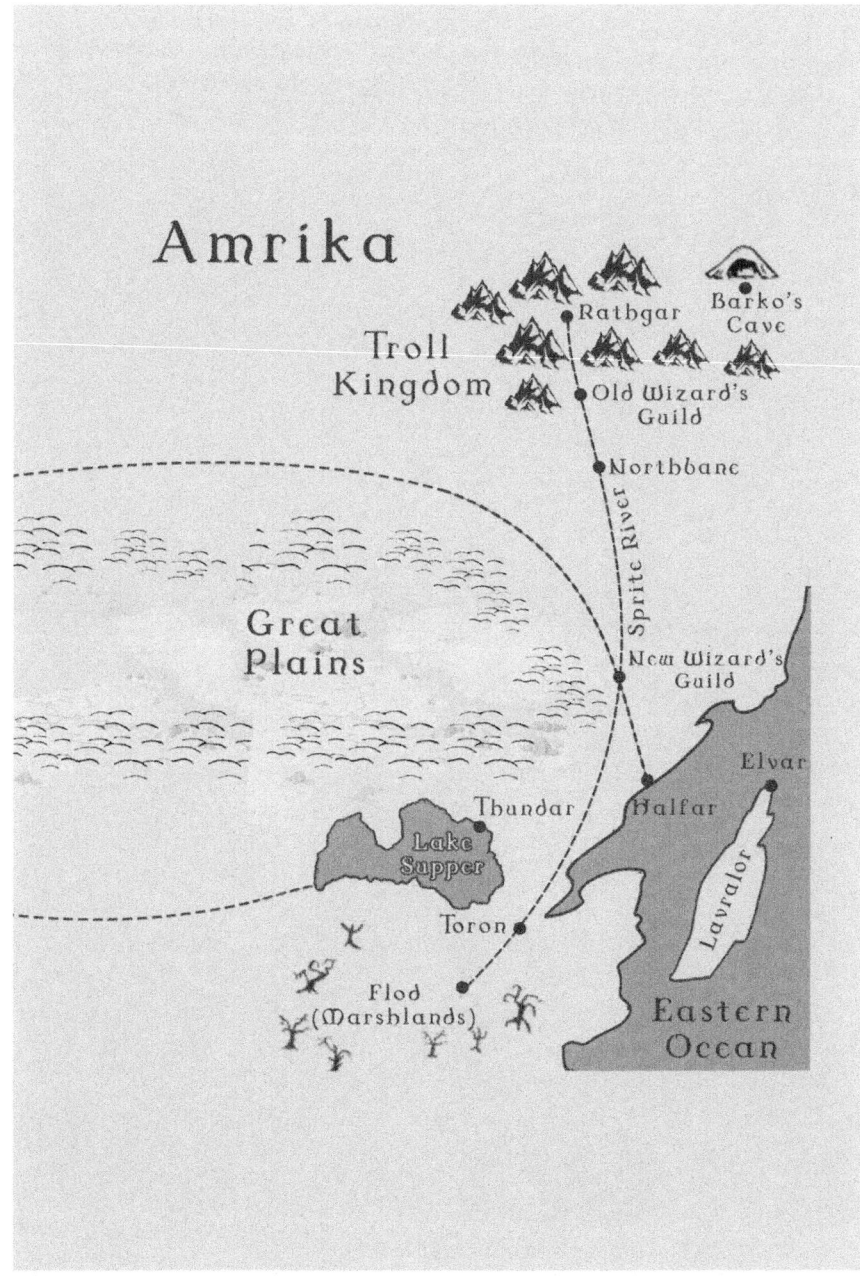

FOREWORD

I read Lord of the Rings as a child. The wonder and escape were like nothing I had ever experienced. I developed a voracious appetite for fantasy and owe many thanks to the influence of the late Terry Goodkind, Terry Brooks, Raymond E. Feist, Tad Williams, J.K. Rowling, Robert Jordan, and David Eddings, to name a few. Fantasy can provide us with simple entertainment and escapism, but it goes deeper than that. It provides different perspectives, explores themes such as the power of friendship, love, and honour, evokes a sense of wonder, lets us partake in adventures we can only dream about, and teaches us valuable truths to apply in our own lives. More importantly, it allows us to imagine. Albert Einstein said, "Imagination is more important than knowledge."

I have wanted to write this series for a long time. It returns to the roots of the pure, epic fantasy I grew up with. I have had the good fortune to achieve the highest success in life, but more importantly, the lowest. The latter is a better teacher than the former. I draw from a rich well. I will let you know that beautiful people exist at both ends. Remember, we are all in this together.

The weapons master once said, "Everything you want is on the other side of fear." I took his advice and put pen to paper. In essence,

I broke through my Wall. I hope this book provides all the benefits mentioned above, and more. I never thought that writing fantasy would be more rewarding than reading it. The inspiration and creativity I experienced were more than I could have dreamed of but made possible because I learned how to imagine.

I hope this story connects and makes a difference in your life because, after all, I wrote it for you.

Sincerely,

Terry Ironwood

This book is dedicated to fantasy readers worldwide. You make it all possible.

1

The orphan stood on the valley rim, bathed in golden afternoon sunlight, gazing at the beautiful kingdom far below in the green valley.

For a moment, Chip felt like the king of the world. He let out a whooping laugh and gathered the image in his arms, cradling it in a loving embrace that he would never let go. Yet he did, in time. The boy opened his eyes, smiling, and studied the beautiful towers and colourful pennants of Vanalon.

It was a small kingdom, as such things go, encircled by the treacherous Grey Mountains. Vanalon's purpose was to guard humankind's westernmost point, the Pass of Death.

Chip turned around to study the fabled pass, nestled between two imposing peaks. He shivered, thinking what might lie beyond, but took comfort knowing that his Manhood Quest ended there.

In truth, Chip was the furthest thing from a king. He was an orphan. The boy did not even have a last name. Born sixteen summers ago and left at the gates of Vanalon, nobody knew where he came from. Villagers who could not conceive would have adopted the boy, but the child possessed a feature no one wanted.

He was born with red eyes.

As the story went, King Barton of Vanalon had squinted at the red-eyed babe brought before him, while gnawing on a chicken leg squeezed in his meaty hand. Holding the shivering infant, the squire asked in a quavering voice, "Where should I take the child?"

The king, who had disappeared behind a flagon of wine, reappeared to shout to the guards. "Feed the baby to the wolves for all I care. Its red eyes are unnatural. Get rid of the cursed thing!"

That might have been the end of Chip, but for the good grace of Queen Charlotte.

She raised one hand to the guards and rested the other on King Barton's arm. "Dear, let's give the child a chance to prove himself," she said in a quiet, measured tone. "When he is old enough, the boy can work as kitchen help in exchange for the great kindness of allowing his life to continue. He can stay in the storage room at the back of the pantry. Besides, abandoning an innocent baby, red eyes or not, to a pack of mountain wolves would not be in the kingdom's best interests. After all, we are not barbarians."

For a moment, Barton was going to reiterate his command, but he made the mistake of glancing at the queen and froze. The king knew that look. The queen rarely interrupted him, especially at dinner, but when she did, it was far easier to agree to her recommendations. Otherwise, he would have to weather her anger for days or weeks afterwards.

After seeing her stony expression, King Barton squinted again at the mewling, red-eyed babe in the squire's arms. He looked back at the bountiful feast in front of him and, with a nod of his bulbous head, gestured that it be so. The queen's lips turned in a self-satisfied smile, and she bowed out of the throne room to let the king finish his meal.

Charlotte hurried down the hall and slipped through the door to the tallest tower of the keep. The petite woman swiftly ascended hundreds of circular stone steps until she reached a large room at the top, the pigeon coop. The queen scribbled a message and tied it to the leg of her favourite pigeon. She released the bird out the open window, watching it disappear into the horizon.

Chip did not know it at the time, but that message would change the course of his life.

After Queen Charlotte saved him, she commanded that they place the baby under the care of the head midwife, Auntie Clare, who loved him despite his red eyes. She named him Chip, saying it just came to her one day.

After only six months at the castle, a remarkable thing happened. Chip's eyes changed from red to forest green. The other midwives had shunned the baby, but after the change, they proclaimed him rid of his evil spirit. Auntie Clare cared for him until he was eight, at which point he was old enough to work in the kitchens.

Initially, kitchen mistress Miss Stern refused to lose her storage room to an orphan boy of all things, especially one born a demon by her account. She was a tall, skeletal woman with grey-streaked black hair tied tightly in a bun. She looked down at the boy with open disdain. "Take him elsewhere," she ordered, "I will not lose a perfectly good storage room to a bastard child born with red eyes. There's a reason someone dumped the unnatural thing in front of the gates. Besides, it is unlikely I could train it properly. It looks too small to do a proper job."

Chip had never seen Auntie Clare get mad or even raise her voice. The head midwife stomped up to Miss Stern with clenched hands and snarled, "The boy is staying in the storage room under orders from the queen herself. You will train him as kitchen help in a dignified manner. His name is Chip, not 'It.' You can defy a royal command at your own peril if you do not like it." The kitchen mistress was taken aback momentarily by Auntie Clare's ferocity, but she hardened her face, and looked down her long nose. It seemed like she might attack the small midwife, but then her expression changed.

"Very well. I will work the boy as the queen commanded," Miss Stern said, smiling icily.

"Good. I will come by to check on him." Auntie Claire unclenched her hands and turned to the boy. She held his small shoulders. Chip desperately wanted to stay with her, but she had fought hard for him to be there. He did not understand why he had to work in the kitchens but would do anything to make her happy. He pressed his lips together so they would not tremble.

"I know this is a big change, but Queen Charlotte wants you to help the kitchen staff," she reassured. "They will teach you new things. It will be alright. I will see you soon." She looked at him with wet eyes and hugged him tightly.

He buried his face in her shoulder, holding back tears. She had been his whole world for the first eight years of his life. He did not want to let her go. She finally held him at arm's length, cupped his cheeks, and kissed his forehead. Auntie Clare glanced coldly at the kitchen mistress, then took leave.

Upon the head midwife's departure, Miss Stern dumped the boy in the dirty storage room at the back of the pantry, old mops and all. She threw a soiled blanket on the cold stone floor for his bedding. "Sleep on this. It's more than you deserve. Use the mop buckets for bathing. You will report for work every day at dawn, with no exceptions."

She stood in the doorway and raised a bony finger. "You are lucky to have a respectable job in the palace for one born of such low station. If I see any manifestation of evil from your demonic side, it will lead to banishment, mark my words. I am keeping an eye on you. You can be sure of that, It."

She glanced around the filthy, windowless room. "Leave the door open for light. I do not trust you with a lantern. The rats will come out at night, but you should fit right in." She spun on her heel, back straight, and slipped out the pantry door. Chip stood for a long time in the center of the small, dark room. He had never felt so alone.

The orphan found sleep difficult that first night. He lay on one half of the small blanket and covered himself with the other. It was wet and smelled. The temperature dropped throughout the late autumn evening, and he found himself shivering. Then the noises started.

He could hear something scurrying around in the pantry and sometimes in the storage room. Louder noises came from the kitchen. Tiny, furry things crawled over him, and he would wake with a start, frantically swiping his body and shaking out the blanket. A tiny sliver of light from a lone lantern in the kitchen peeked under the pantry door, but it only made him see shadows moving about.

He closed his eyes tight and thought of his small bed in the head midwife's quarters and the soothing fire banked low in the hearth. He realized that life was now gone.

He knew nobody owed him anything. Most people shunned him and wanted nothing to do with him. He would try to get used to this new life and make the best of it. He did not want to upset Auntie Clare, so he wouldn't complain. With that thought at the forefront of his mind, he dozed off, still shivering.

"It!" a sharp voice called. Chip sat up straight and raised his hand to ward off the bright light. Dawn had arrived. Miss Stern stood silhouetted in the doorway in a dark dress, bony hands on her hips. "Get up now. What did I tell you? When the rooster crows, you must be ready to work." Even as she said the words, he could make out the faint sound of the birds proclaiming dawn through the stone walls. "Your new name is It. If you even think of telling your fake mother that you are mistreated, I will take away all the nice things I have done for you. No light, no blanket, and no food for starters. I can be strict if need be, so do not test me."

She grabbed a dusty broom propped against the wall and jabbed him. "Hurry up. If you do this again tomorrow, I will lock you in all day with no food or water." He leapt to his feet and brushed his brown hair down with his fingers. In disgust, he saw spiders and other things run into the shadows away from the light. She waved him forward into the kitchen.

It was then that the nightmare truly began.

For two years, she tormented the boy with menial jobs, ensuring he received the worst tasks. His life consisted of scrubbing pots and pans, mopping floors, fetching water, and emptying the latrines. The kitchen staff looked down on him with contempt, for he was a lowly orphan in their eyes.

Chip lost weight and grew little during this period. The boy was already small and thought, at times, that he would never grow. He tried to stay happy but found it increasingly difficult.

Auntie Clare came to see him when she could, but the kitchen mistress put the orphan on a gruelling schedule that left him no free time. When he saw her, his small face lit up, and he was flooded with warm memories. They would walk briefly in the garden, and she would ask after him, a look of concern in her eyes. He always told her that everything was fine, even trying to smile. Each time she left, his heart sank, but he put on a brave face and wouldn't cry until he was alone in his room in the dark.

By age ten, the boy's rib cage showed, and his face had grown gaunt. Chip felt hopelessness permeate his entire life. He grew weaker and moved slower, which infuriated Miss Stern further. "Move faster, It!" she would scream, and he did.

One day, he was completely exhausted and dragged his feet. He knew something was wrong with him inside. His body was having trouble responding. It was the end of another gruelling day, and he was the last person still working. He could barely hold up the mop.

Miss Stern appeared behind him. "This should have been done a long time ago, It, and you missed a spot. No food again tonight. I have been far too lenient with you. Now move faster, It!"

The kitchen mistress shoved him, and he accidentally dropped the mop, knocking a glass off the counter that shattered on the floor. He looked at the mess and turned to her with wide eyes, cringing. Miss Stern struck him hard across the face, sending the orphan sprawling across the cold stone floor. Bits of glass embedded in his face and hands as he slid. Chip felt a sharp pain.

It was the first time he had felt anything in a long while, and something broke inside the boy. Amidst the pain of the slap, Chip felt a release. An incredible rage engulfed him, one he had bottled for far too long. He got to his feet with his back to Miss Stern, standing there with fists clenched at his sides, energized with a nearly uncontrollable fury.

She was about to strike him again, but he turned to face her. According to Miss Stern, the boy's eyes blazed bright red. She shrieked in fear and ran screaming from the kitchen, claiming later that he had defied a direct order and tried to strike her.

The guards brought the child before the king and queen at Miss Stern's behest. She claimed he was a demon and wanted him removed from the kitchen or, even better, banished from the castle.

"Come forward, boy," the king had commanded from a large ornate wooden table in the throne room. Beside him, the queen looked concerned. Chip shuffled forward. He looked thin and sallow, small even for a ten-year-old. His face was bruised and cut. He remembered not caring what happened to him at that point.

"Look at me!" the king barked. The queen shifted uncomfortably. Chip raised his head. Besides the bruises and cuts, his face was stark white with dark circles under his green eyes. The king snorted. "Your eyes may be green now, boy, but I have no reason to disbelieve Miss Stern. If you are a demon, I imagine it is easy to change your eye colour at will. Trying to strike our kitchen mistress is grounds for lashing, even banishment."

Miss Stern, standing to the side, nodded in appreciation.

The queen tried to intervene. "He is just a boy, Barton, and by his physical state, overworked or ill. Let us give him some rest for a few days. Perhaps we can send him to the laundress, where he might fit in better."

She patted the king's arm and smiled.

Barton looked incredulous.

"Tolerating insubordination will set a precedent that I refuse to let fester." The queen was about to respond, but he held up a meaty hand. "Not this time, Charlotte. This orphan is cursed and carries a demon in him. He is hiding his true self as we speak. Give him fifty lashings, then set him on the One Road. The boy can assume his true form then or die as the Creator wills."

Charlotte tried to intercede, but he held up a finger. She bowed her head in dejection.

Chip stood forlornly in the middle of the throne room, looking down as the king pronounced his sentence. He felt like laughing, unable to care anymore, and so weak he could barely stand. His little waiflike body rocked to and fro.

He felt as lonely a boy as there ever was.

"Any last words before your lashings and banishment?" the king asked, smiling with satisfaction as the poor orphan swayed.

Chip raised his chin and, without flinching, met King Barton's eyes. For a moment, he was not going to respond, but then the boy felt something stir. It was a festering anger he'd been having trouble containing since his episode with Miss Stern.

"I never chose this," he started quietly. "My parents abandoned me. If I had red eyes at birth, it was not my fault. I am happy with Auntie Clare, who is like a mother to me. She is loving and kind. I thank Queen Charlotte for that. I followed Miss Stern's orders when they sent me to the kitchen. She made me work from dawn til bedtime without a break every day for the last two years." The boy raised his voice. "I don't know a lot of people, but she is the wickedest person I know."

Miss Stern stepped forward with a gasp. "See what an evil little..."

The king held up his hand.

"Let the boy speak. I want to hear what this demon has to say." He leaned forward. "Go on. Say your last words."

The chair he drooped over squeaked as the large man shifted his weight.

Chip cast a hateful gaze at Miss Stern.

"You hit me in the face because I wasn't moving fast enough after a full day's work. I never tried to hit you, but now I wish I had. You are a mean, ugly, old witch." The kitchen mistress's mouth opened, but nothing came out. Chip then locked eyes with the king. "I'm not a demon, and I have no powers," he said, his voice becoming louder. "Miss Stern is lying to you. Lash me if you want, and banish me. I do not want to be part of your stupid kingdom anymore anyway. You are not fit to be a king!"

Everyone in the room froze. The king sat slack-jawed. The queen covered her mouth. The squire behind the king simply passed out. After an initial moment of pure shock, Barton's face became beet red with rage. He stood on shaky legs, pointing a trembling finger at the boy who now had a grin on his face!

The king's voice, hoarse at first, turned into a scream. "You dare talk to me in that manner! Guards! Chop off..." Someone cleared their throat loudly. The king trailed off, looking sideways. Appearing from the shadows at the side of the throne room, the wizard Xander strode forward with his Protector, weapons master Garth Stone.

The wizard bowed slightly to the king. "Begging your pardon, King Barton, but before pronouncing judgment in this matter, I would like to intercede upon the boy's behalf."

He glanced at the orphan, who stared in wonder at Xander.

Ten years before, the wizard and his Protector had arrived, declaring Vanalon their home. High Wizard Balor, Xander's older brother, had asked them to keep an eye on the Pass of Death and provide guidance to the newly crowned King, Barton. Even High King Dominor, King Barton's uncle from the capital city of Toron, blessed the mission.

Chip could only gaze in wonder as he looked upon the legend of so many stories. Xander winked at the boy before turning back to the king. It was the first time he had ever acknowledged the orphan.

"I would hear your words, Grand Wizard Xander," the king intoned formally as he sat back down, making an obvious effort to control himself.

"First and foremost," the wizard began in a matter-of-fact tone, "the boy is not a demon. To suggest otherwise would insult my powers honed over a lifetime of experience and study. Second, banishing a small boy in the cold amongst superstitious villagers who believe in this falsehood is akin to a death sentence. Have the descendants of the great kings of Amrika reduced themselves to sentencing children to death for an unproven tantrum?"

His eyes looked piercingly at the king, who seemed to shrink. Few men in the land of Amrika could long hold that gaze.

"I... did not think it was a concern to you," the king stammered, still shocked by the interruption. Xander rarely intervened in or discussed mundane matters. The guards in the throne room were still mouthing questions to each other, asking how the wizard had arrived unnoticed.

"It is now," Xander said, turning to the orphan. "The red eyes were likely a birth defect that has resolved itself, but I would like to study him further. As punishment for his outburst, I advise you to hand the boy over to my Protector, Garth Stone. Instead of lashings or banishment, the weapons master will train him harder than anyone in the kingdom. That, I can assure you, is punishment enough. In addition, I ask that he be allowed to attend school as the training of the body goes hand in hand with the mind."

The king squirmed in his chair. "Uh... I still think it prudent to err on the side of caution here and set a proper example, so unless you insist..."

"I insist," the wizard said quietly.

Beneath bushy white eyebrows, Xander's eyes bore into King Barton. That penetrating gaze housed unfathomable power and wisdom if even a fraction of the tales were true.

The king gulped. "Of course, Grand Wizard Xander, as you wish. If he is not a demon, we should make a man of him yet," he declared it as if it was his idea. "Strict training and discipline will achieve this goal. Under normal circumstances, I would hang him for insulting a king, but we shall blame it on ignorance and illness. Give him to the weapons master," he said, waving his hand.

Miss Stern stepped forward, her skeletal face enraged. "He insulted you, my king. The boy must be punished further!"

The wizard extended his hand without turning. Miss Stern shrieked as her feet left the ground and she flew across the floor to stop inches from the wizard's face. The air crackled with magic. Chip gasped in wonder, feeling the energy in his bones. Xander's eyes were blazing bright blue.

"The king has already pronounced judgment, Miss Stern. Consider yourself lucky you are not banished for almost working a child to death. The boy can barely stand. If he does not survive this illness, I will take a personal interest in you. The king has put laws in place that regulate the behaviours of his staff. The punishment for breaching these laws is severe. Did you want to continue? If so, I am all ears."

The wizard smiled broadly, showing a full mouth of gleaming white teeth, but his eyes held no mirth. Instead, they were filled with a blazing blue intensity that roiled with incredible power. Miss Stern's mouth opened and closed. She shook her head.

The wizard released her with an almost imperceptible wave of his hand. She flew back and landed heavily in a chair. With a slight bow to the king, who sat open-mouthed, Xander put an arm around the boy's shoulders and ushered him out of the throne room, his Protector in tow.

2

The weapons master, Garth Stone, took the boy under his care, creating a comfortable room in the stables. The sparse furnishings included straw bedding, several blankets, and a night table. During the first few days, Garth focused only on the child's health, feeding him warm soup and bits of toast.

Unfortunately, the orphan's condition deteriorated. His fever increased, so Garth dumped him in a tub of cool water. Chip was so sick that he barely noticed. This concerned the weapons master who sent for the wizard. Xander arrived shortly after and assessed the situation through narrowed eyes.

"He has no strength left to fight the fever alone," the wizard spoke gravely. "He will not survive the night."

Xander reached into his robes and produced a small vial. He tried to pour a drop onto Chip's tongue, but the boy clutched the wizard's hand. His small face was stark white, and his lips were turning blue. "It's alright... let me go. I should never... have been born. Nobody wants me..."

The boy's hand fell away.

The wizard stared at the dying child with great concern, and rested a hand on the orphan's forehead. Xander's eyes turned bright blue and the air crackled with raw power.

The wizard began to shake. "He is fighting me. He does not want to live anymore. Such strength..." He gasped in astonishment. "The cold caress is taking hold of him. Death is turning this way." His eyes widened. "I can see the Divide between Life and Death. There is no time." He put both hands on Chip's forehead. "I must give him a reason to live."

Xander directed thoughts of comfort to the boy. The older man included memories of his own adventures, sharing images of exotic places and beautiful cities. The wizard thought of exciting people he had met over the years who had intrigued and inspired him. He even showed the orphan bits of his childhood, including the struggles he'd endured to achieve his remarkable success.

It was not working.

Chip had made up his mind. Vast, crushing hopelessness radiated from the stubborn boy. The child showed the wizard his suffering for the last two years, his bleak orphan past, and his equally bleak future. When an image of Miss Stern appeared, a rage ignited in the boy that stunned the wizard. Yet even that hatred was not enough to bring him back.

Knowing time was running out, the wizard prodded Chip's memories until he found one of Auntie Clare, drawing a hint of joy. The wizard seized on this and emblazoned the image of the head midwife, beckoning him towards the beautiful world of life. He pulled memories of her making jokes, playing frivolous games, and caring for him. He latched on to an image of the boy sitting on her lap in front of a roaring fire, mesmerized by a tall tale. With time running out, the old man pulled up a powerful final memory of her hugging him tightly. Chip finally responded, and his image turned away from death's cold darkness.

Sadly, it was too late.

A black thing that could only be Death saw him and would not let go. The dark being reached through the Divide, dragging him in. Xander instinctively averted his eyes from Death's gaze lest he be pulled in too. Not even the wizard's formidable strength could save the boy. With immeasurable sadness, he sent Chip a comforting thought wishing him peace in the afterworld.

The boy's body went into spasms as he died.

Then something strange happened.

THE COLD, unnatural touch of Death shocked Chip out of his depression and misery. With stunning clarity, its touch showed him the preciousness of life. In his mind, the boy turned towards the presence of Xander and again examined the wizard's memories. He realized how much he had not experienced in his short life. He yearned to go on adventures and see those exotic places. He longed to roam the lands and meet new people. He desired to love and be loved. The orphan decided he wanted to live, after all. Even more, he promised himself never to give up again. Chip gave his word. Death could wait.

The boy turned and stared directly into the face of Death. He uttered a word, and his eyes blazed a bright red. The dark, shapeless being recoiled, allowing the Divide between Life and Death to snap back in place. A lingering howl of rage echoed across the emptiness.

THE WIZARD FLEW backward and struck the wall. Chip trembled and became still. Xander scrambled to his feet and rushed to the boy, lifting his eyelids. The eyes beneath were green, not red. The wizard scowled and looked at the orphan's chest, which was now moving up and down at a slow, steady pace. The boy's face appeared calm and, unless the old man was mistaken, displayed a hint of a grin.

Xander, still wobbly from the ordeal, looked at the weapons master. "His mind is different. He... stayed Death itself. His eyes... Could it be?" He paused, his face inscrutable. "I must leave now to find some truths, journeying to a place I should have gone to long ago." The wizard sighed. "In truth, I was always afraid to..." His eyes grew distant, and then he refocused on his Protector. "I must go alone."

The weapons master was about to protest, but the wizard held up his hand and went on, "Even your mighty sword can not help me in this place. The boy will recover. Stay here and nurse him to health, then begin his training. I will be back by winter's solstice, the Creator willing."

The weapons master nodded.

With that, the wizard turned and was gone.

Chip rested for two weeks as he recovered from his illness and began to gain weight. He did not remember the events of the night when the wizard helped heal him.

Garth provided the boy with delicious soups and stews made special from the kitchen. Miss Stern seemed to have a vested interest in ensuring the boy fully recovered. She bent over backwards to provide whatever meals the weapons master requested. Chip knew she was only striving to avoid the wizard's wrath, which made him smile.

"Your body will be trained when it recovers," instructed Garth. "Your mental training, which is more important, will begin now."

The weapons master was a man of few words, but those he spoke were important and measured. He proceeded to describe the mental arts of combat and living. The boy focused on each saying, trying hard to internalize the lesson.

"Everything you want is on the other side of fear."

"You only grow through discomfort."

"Everything in life is a challenge."

Garth continued to repeat these truths to the healing boy. He elaborated when questioned and sometimes included a story to emphasize the lesson.

After two weeks had passed, Garth instructed Chip to be ready for physical training in the yard. He taught him the basics of weaponry, conditioning, and hand-to-hand combat. At all times, he reiterated his fundamental truths of life.

By the end of the first week of training, Chip could barely walk or lift his arms. They had drilled mercilessly with weighty wooden practice swords. Over and over, he rehearsed different patterns. Every muscle throbbed in pain.

Garth Stone was relentless. He commanded the boy to go through endless drills, patterns, and exercises. The man immediately addressed any mistakes in form or decision-making. Sometimes, the weapons master would practice beside him with a real sword, moving so fast Chip could barely register his speed. It was a blur of motion and then a silhouette when he completed his pattern. This, of course, made Chip feel as slow as a sloth bear.

Praise was rare, but that's what made it so valuable. He learned to seek out acknowledgement, no matter how small, which gave him a sense of worth and fulfillment. The weapons master became a role model, something he'd never had.

Chip redoubled his efforts, pushing away the pain and fatigue. Garth observed intently, his face unreadable.

By the end of the second week, the orphan finally stumbled and fell after another gruelling day of practice. The weapons master stood to the side with arms folded.

"When you feel you can't go on, you have lots left."

Chip thought about it as he gasped for air, then nodded. The boy gritted his teeth and pushed himself off the ground, waiting for further instruction. Garth studied him momentarily, then turned and strode out of the yard.

"We begin again at dawn."

The orphan thought for the briefest moment that he detected a subtle grin but couldn't be sure. He stumbled back to the stable and collapsed on his cot. The child was asleep in moments.

The third week proved the most challenging. Garth increased the training intensity to the point where each day was harder than the last. Chip reminded himself that he always had lots left. This served him well, but by the end of the third week, he realized that the human body could only take so much. Everything had limits, didn't it?

On the last day of the week, Garth spent the whole afternoon sparring with him. He was ruthless. Attack after attack came until the boy's lungs screamed in agony, and his limbs throbbed. The weapons master did not relent. "Again."

Chip dug deep and responded every time, until the final time.

The sun was beginning to set as Garth executed a blistering attack that he parried with his last bit of strength. The final blow came in slow motion. He tried to raise his sword, but his body would not respond. Instead, the practice blade slipped from numb fingers, and his body fell backwards.

All the while, he watched the weapons master swing a full two-handed overhead blow towards his skull. He realized he had nothing left to give. The feeling of shame that enveloped him was more painful than the blow that was about to strike his head and likely end his short life. Chip resigned himself to the fact that he had reached his limit. The boy braced himself for the impact as the wooden blade whistled through the air.

Then it stopped.

Garth Stone stood over his prone body with the sword motionless a hair's breadth above his head. He looked at him for a long moment, grunted and threw the sword off to the side.

Chip realized he had failed him. "I gave up. I'm sorry."

Garth Stone assessed his condition. "You must learn the greatest truth of all. Never give up!" he said, starting to walk away.

Chip scowled. *Go figure*, he thought. He then tried to make an excuse. "I just can't ..."

Garth rounded on him.

"Don't make excuses, and never use the word 'can't,'" the weapons master instructed, cutting him short. "Here." He scrawled a message with a quill pen on some parchment from his waist pouch and handed it over. "Take this to the baths. They will soak you in water with salts and a few other herbs, as per my instructions. You are still weak. Training is always the hardest in the beginning. We grow when we rest, so enjoy this small comfort. In two days, we continue."

Garth began striding from the yard, then stopped and turned.

Chip managed to rise to a sitting position, though he was still breathing hard.

"I needed to see your limits. Now you know them as well. Understand that limits are not real." Garth paused, and for once, the lines in his face relaxed. "You did well."

He turned and left the yard.

Chip stared after him for a moment, then despite everything, laughed aloud. His body and mind felt broken, but now he understood the lesson. Now he knew where he stood. Despite his exhaustion, the boy let out a whoop of joy. He had done well!

Chip realized he was still holding the message in his hand. He read it out loud and thought of a nice warm bath. He had heard of the bathhouse but never thought they would permit entrance to someone of his station. It was usually reserved for the garrison officers, the master smith, or the stable master. The orphan forced himself to a standing position, then limped off, groaning in pain.

The bathhouse was a large stone structure attached to the side of the palace. Several chimneys vented steam and heat from the tiled roof. When the small boy arrived, he struggled to open the heavyset door. Everything hurt. Chip entered with trepidation, unsure what to expect.

It was a cold autumn evening, but many candles bathed the foyer in warm light. The hostess sat in the small anteroom at a polished wooden desk. He was not used to such a formal place. When she asked for his errand, he handed her the note. After she read the message and noticed who'd signed it, the woman stood up immediately and waved him forward. He passed through an oak door behind the desk and followed her down a long passage with rooms on either side. Steam mixed with the aroma of scented soap filled the air.

She stopped by a cabinet in the hallway and pulled out several small bags. The woman ushered him into a medium-sized room with an elaborate bathtub full of steaming water. A square soap bar lay beside the tub on a polished silver dish. Rich cedar planks covered the walls. He had never seen such luxury. When he lived in the storage room off the pantry, his bath consisted of a bucket of boiled water with some not-so-nice-smelling soap. This place, by contrast, made him feel like a king.

The hostess explained that his soiled clothes needed to go in the basket by the door. When finished with his bath, he could wrap himself in one of the cushy bathrobes hanging on the wall. A padded leather chair was in the corner of the room beside a small table with several sheaves of parchment if he desired to read while drying off. She poured the contents of the small bags into the tub and then excused herself.

Chip noticed a heady, herby scent permeate the air. Eager to test the water, he undressed and deposited his clothes in the proper basket by the door. When he entered the tub, the hot water infused his aching muscles. The boy stretched out in sheer joy and breathed in the steaming herbs.

A slight knock at the door jolted him upright, and a moment later, the hostess took away his clothes. She closed the door, and he settled back down. Chip had no idea what they would do with his clothes and did not care. At that moment, he just floated in restful ecstasy.

The boy lost track of time until he heard another slight knock. The hostess slid a basket in with his clothes washed, dried, and folded. She pulled the door shut. Chip climbed out, put on the oversized robe, and sat on the padded chair, imagining he was a high-level officer or captain. He pretended to give commands to ordinary soldiers. The orphan pictured an army of trolls attacking the capital city of Toron as he stood on the walls issuing orders. He had no idea what either looked like but he imagined high walls and fearsome creatures.

Standing up in his cushy robe, the boy brandished a sword only he could see as he stood victorious on the battlefield. He then kneeled as High King Dominor placed a wreath on his head and thanked him for saving the city. Chip grinned at the image.

The idea of being important was difficult to imagine, but it felt comforting. The boy latched on to the hope that if he worked and trained hard enough, he might one day become a common soldier who earned a small salary. People might forget he was an orphan and a baby born with red eyes. He knew it was a big dream, but the weapons master had stressed the importance of setting and visualizing goals.

The herbs in the water had worked their magic, and his muscles felt rejuvenated. Chip dressed and left with a smile, feeling refreshed. Two days later, he resumed training and received some new truths.

"Good habits make you strong."

"Strike first if it is not expected."

"Fighting is the easy part if you've trained enough."

The weapons master continued training the boy, but only on evenings and weekends. He explained that the first three weeks had been a test to see his perceived limits. By pushing his body to its breaking point, Chip created a valuable memory that he could use to sustain him in all areas of his life. Everything would be easier and achievable because of it. Besides, the man had other duties to attend to. Under the wizard's advice, the king had instated Garth as commander of the entire garrison.

During the day, the weapons master trained the two hundred or so men who guarded the small kingdom, drilling the soldiers and officers in the yard. Chip soon realized that Garth Stone was superior to all. The soldiers addressed him as 'High Commander of Vanalon.' The men respected and deferred to him on any training issues or defence tactics.

Chip overheard soldiers talking in the stable about Garth's reputation in the Capital, Toron. In awed voices, they whispered about how he was considered the greatest Sword Master in all Amrika, which was why Xander chose him as his Protector. They knew the Grand Wizard was second only to his older brother, High Wizard Balor, in magic. To have a great wizard and swordsman in the tiny kingdom of Vanalon was an honour.

When Garth trained alongside the boy in the evenings, Chip could only marvel at his speed and power. He was taller than most men and appeared chiselled from granite. The man only ever wore black. He had bits of gray in his dark hair at his temples but still looked middle-aged. Getting anywhere near the weapons master's skill level seemed virtually impossible to the orphan.

One night was particularly frustrating, and he grumbled that life was unfair. Garth Stone spun around.

"Life is not fair." He let the words sink in. "Understand that some people have greater challenges than others. And try not to blame anyone for your misfortune."

Chip experienced confusion at the statement. Surely, people were to blame for things.

The weapons master noticed his expression and elaborated. "Blame can lead to hate and freeze your growth. It is understandable to blame others, but don't use it to make excuses and not take responsibility for your own actions. Those who hurt us should and will be held accountable by our laws and perhaps by the Creator. However, punishment should usually err on the side of mercy to improve them, for they, too, have likely been wronged. If blame is keeping you prisoner, seek to forgive, for only then can you be truly free. Life is not fair and never will be. When it feels unfair, look at it as a challenge. It is necessary to accept this."

Chip thought about it. "I think I understand. Just don't call me "It.""

"It?" Garth arched an eyebrow.

"Miss Stern called me that. I don't really look like an "It," do I?" The boy broke out into a grin.

The weapons master grunted. "You were unfairly treated as a child, no doubt. In the Wizard's Guild, where I was trained to become a Protector, we were told to thank anyone who wronged us. It is drastic, but it teaches us to look at things differently. People who wrong us can cause us to grow and learn if we look at it as a challenge. Miss Stern did not treat you well, but it caused you to learn self-control and appreciate the small things. It made you resilient. In the end, despite her flaws, she is still human and bears her own burdens. It may not be easy, but try to let go of blame and learn to forgive. It is for your sake, not theirs. Set yourself free."

Chip's eyes widened. He had never thought about looking at

others that way. He hated Miss Stern, but a weight seemed to lift off his shoulders when he realized the futility of blame. He would never want to suffer again as he did, but if he thought about it, he did grow from the experience, even though it almost killed him. It made him appreciate everything he had now, even small things like a candle or a blanket. Life was not fair. The orphan may have been handed a sad lot in life, but he would consider it an opportunity to grow. He felt a sense of relief and freedom.

The boy sighed.

"And I won't call you 'It,'" Garth said with a straight face.

Chip looked to see if he was serious. The Weapons master broke into a rare smile and started walking away. "That's all for today."

The orphan grinned and went to bed that evening with a lighter heart.

His training continued, and the weeks passed. Chip absorbed the mental truths repeated to him daily, changing his outlook on the world. He found it surprising that a few simple truths could change his viewpoint, but it was important to repeat them daily. Despite the hard work, he found an inner peace and happiness that gave him hope.

After a couple of months of training, the weapons master told him to go to school in the mornings instead of doing stable work. It was the first time he would ever be around other children.

The school was a standalone structure inside the palace walls, separate from the main buildings. All the children of the staff and high-ranking officers, including the prince and princess themselves, attended this private school.

Chip made sure to clean his best tunic the night before, which had only one hole in it. His brown hair was neatly combed.

The boy arrived that morning with no small amount of trepidation. The other children milling about in the yard ranged in age from eight to sixteen summers, neatly dressed. Most seemed to exude an air of superiority. Chip, a scrawny ten-year-old orphan, felt out of place.

"Are you the orphan demon?" a large boy demanded, walking up to him. His clothes looked to be made of velvet with beautiful, stitched symbols. Three others of equal size accompanied him.

Chip expected to be treated differently because of his status, but the comment surprised him.

"The demon probably can't even speak, Rupert!" chortled the boy on the right. "He has never been to school, so what do you expect? He can't read or write either, just like most commoners."

Chip's eyes widened. The boy in front of him must be Prince Rupert, the only son of King Barton. He knew the prince was two years older and reminded him of a wiggly, large baby pig. He had his father's flabby jowls.

"I can do all three," Chip said calmly. "Auntie Clare taught me."

"Who... you mean the old midwife?" Rupert sneered. "I remember now. She reared you as a pup instead of throwing you to the wolves where you belong. I heard the kitchen kicked you out because your demon eyes went red. I dare you to try that with us."

"I'm not a demon," Chip said flatly, standing his ground.

"You may train with the commander as punishment, but we aren't afraid of you, demon orphan. You should have stayed behind the barrier where you belong." The prince walked right up to him, looking down. His breath smelled of onions.

"Rupert, get away from him this instant!" A small girl pushed her way between them and turned on the larger boy, waggling a finger. "Mother told us to treat him like everyone else. Do not make me tell on you."

She stared him down with tiny fists on her hips.

The prince looked at her for a long moment, then glanced at Chip and shrugged. He raised his hands in a placating manner. "We were just introducing ourselves. It is important our subjects know who we are. We will keep an eye on him. After all, the safety of Vanalon is everyone's concern. See you around, orphan." He sauntered away with a broad smile. His three friends left with him, snickering.

The little girl turned around and their noses almost touched. He stepped back awkwardly, amazed that the princess of Vanalon was right in front of him.

"I'm Princess Eleanor," she held out her tiny hand.

Chip's eyes widened. He was unsure if he was supposed to kiss or shake it. Both felt wrong for one of his station. Instead, he did the next best thing. He froze, not necessarily of his own volition.

"Uh..." he managed.

"Ha!" she squealed. "You are funny." The princess reached down and shook his hand. "Nice to meet you. I am sorry about my brother. He believes orphans and commoners are beneath him. The word commoner is frowned upon now, thanks to my mother, Queen Charlotte. She believes it's... archaic. Yes, that's the word. It means old fashioned."

Chip had been very nervous, but the princess had a way of making him calm. He also remembered his training, "Everything I want is on the other side of fear."

The boy took a deep breath. "It's alright. A lot of people think I'm... a demon. But I'm not, I swear."

Eleanor laughed hysterically. "Of course you're not. Anyone with half a wit knows that. My mother told us about you. Rupert takes after my father, King Barton. He can be insufferable."

"He's a big oaf," a voice said behind her.

"You got that right," she laughed, turning around.

Chip's eyes widened hearing someone call the prince a name in front of the princess.

A wiry, rambunctious boy his age stood grinning. He was tall with bright blue eyes and light brown hair. "I'm Chase, the squire's son," he proffered a hand. This time, Chip shook it.

"I'm Chip... the orphan.," he said sheepishly, at a loss for words.

"Ha. Good one!" Chase laughed heartily, slapping him on the shoulder. The princess joined in. The bell suddenly rang.

The princess grabbed both boys' hands and ran across the yard to the heavyset doors leading into the school.

From that moment on, they formed an inseparable trio.

Chase, the son of the king's squire, had started school two years before and was likely destined to follow in his father's footsteps, assuming he stayed out of trouble. He was clever, though not bright, and mischievous enough that he never failed to make Chip laugh. They became best friends.

Princess Eleanor and Chase were already friends from before. Together, the three of them made a formidable wall against Prince Rupert, who scowled at them when they put up a united front. The prince was relentless with his quips, but Eleanor would step in as often as possible and scold her overbearing brother. Exasperated, Rupert would stalk off after she planted tiny fists on her hips and gave him a verbal thrashing.

The princess was Chip's age but much smaller, yet she had no problem standing up for him. He loved that about her and appreciated the protection from the taunting prince.

Thirty-one children made up the class taught by the straight-backed Miss Owl, who assigned different lessons based on age. During breaks, the children would form groups and play various games. Chip began to look forward to school in the mornings. It was a welcome break from training.

Grand Wizard Xander returned a day before the winter solstice that year and spoke at length in a hushed voice with the weapons master. Afterwards, he asked to see Chip in his stable room. The boy sat on his cot while the wizard pulled up the only chair in the small room and slumped into it. He had dark circles under his eyes, and his face seemed more lined than usual.

"When your eyes went red with Miss Stern, did you feel anything?" he inquired without delay.

"Only that I was really mad at her," Chip answered. "I also felt very powerful."

"Did you feel anything else in your mind?" the wizard asked, leaning forward.

The boy thought for a long moment. "No, I don't think so. Just that I wanted to hurt her."

The wizard grunted, changing direction. "Do you remember when you were sick, and I placed my hands on your forehead?"

Chip shook his head. The wizard placed a finger on the boy's temple. A memory formed of him shivering in the darkness. Images of different cities and experiences flashed in his mind. The orphan gasped. The wizard watched his reaction.

"I remember."

"Good. Now, do you remember falling into darkness? Take your time."

After several moments, Chip answered, "I was being pulled by something dark and unending. I knew it would have me if I didn't break free."

"Did you feel anything in your mind?" the wizard asked, leaning closer.

"No." Chip looked at him innocently. Xander sat back and sighed. "Wait, yes." The wizard's eyes narrowed. "I could feel something with me. Or it might have always been there, and I couldn't see it before. It was like a great force or... a power. It was hidden behind... I saw an image ..."

"An image of what?" The wizard leaned forward, this time holding his breath.

Chip scrunched his face. "A Wall!"

The wizard exhaled explosively.

"My goodness!" Xander exclaimed, getting up to pace the small room. After several long moments, he finally sat before the boy and put both hands on his temples. "This will not hurt. Relax and close your eyes." Chip felt a presence enter his mind. It was probing for something. He sensed a definite power in Xander, but nothing like the dark thing trying to get him when he had the fever. He could not see the Wall in his mind this time. The wizard finally withdrew his presence.

"I cannot see anything," he said, sighing. The old man wiped his brow wearily. "I am afraid I do not know at this stage. We will see when you are older."

"See what?" Chip asked curiously.

The wizard seemed to mull over how to answer the question. He pulled out a pouch and pipe, inserting a pinch of tobacco in the end, and lit it with a long finger that flared briefly with blue magic. The boy felt a small crackle of energy run through him. Chip's eyes widened at even that tiny display of magic. He found it fascinating. Xander inhaled deeply, blowing out a great plume of smoke that floated up to the rafters. A howl of wind sounded outside. It seemed a winter storm would herald in tomorrow's solstice.

"I suppose I owe you some explanation." The wizard shifted his weight as he crossed his legs, taking a second pull on the pipe. "Listen well. Magic exists in a small number of people. Or it exists in all people, and only a small number can access it. The word 'magic' usually implies trickery or illusion, so it can be misunderstood. I like to call it the Power. Only a small number of people can recognize it, let alone use it. The Power can have devastating consequences if misused or in the wrong hands."

He drew on his pipe as he considered how best to explain. "When practiced, magic or Power cannot be hidden. It always manifests in the eyes of the user and can also be felt or sensed by some, depending on the distance. Wizards have tried to cover their eyes, but that is a telltale sign they have the Power. The weakest Power is yellow, followed by green, brown, blue, and then, in theory, red. There are power differences in the different colours or Levels.

"Those with more Power blaze brighter. Each Level is more attuned to certain types of skills, so a Lower Level can still have much Power even though, in general, they are weaker. For instance, a Yellow can usually heal better than any other colour. A Brown can access wind, water, and earth better than a Blue, who is more adept with wizard fire and more powerful overall. It all comes down to mastery within your Level. The eyes, however, never lie."

Chip listened, mesmerized. He wondered how powerful this old man was.

"Your eyes blazed blue in front of the king when you lifted Miss Stern off the ground. I felt a crackle in the air... an energy," Chip said innocently. Xander choked on his pipe. Bits of smoke trailed out of his mouth between coughs.

"You could feel that?" the wizard asked in shock. The boy nodded. "Watching someone's eyes light up is one thing, but you are not supposed to sense magic until you mature. Not for several years at the earliest. Humans who can feel magic that way are called Sensers. Many of them cannot wield magic themselves. But, all who do wield magic can sense it too, to varying degrees."

Xander sank back in his chair, forehead creased in thought.

"I even felt it when you lit your pipe a few moments ago," Chip added with a grin. The wizard coughed again.

"My goodness. You should not be able to sense a small use of magic like that unless you are very powerful." He appraised the small boy again. "The Power shines brighter in accordance with how much is used. My eyes only shine a little when lighting a small pipe. Feeling or sensing the small magic used to light a pipe is very difficult. The stories of your red eyes have me the most perplexed. I would be even more skeptical if I had not seen it in your mind."

"What did you see?" Chip asked in wonder. He was happy that someone was taking an interest in him, let alone a powerful wizard. If the boy could sense magic, he would know when anyone used their Power around him, even if he could not use it himself. That way, Chip did not have to see their eyes. He would feel it. *That would be fun*, the boy thought.

"In your fever, Death saw you, or the entity we call Death. Some call it the Darkness. It is a force that no one really understands, but in the end, we all succumb to it. Death began to pull you over the boundary or Divide into his icy embrace. I found it disturbing that he could reach through the Divide like that. I did not think it was possible."

The wizard paused as he mulled over the ramifications. He shrugged and studied the boy once again. "Not even my Power could save you. I had to let go lest he pull me in too. Then you turned to him, eyes blazing red, and uttered a word." The wizard shook his head in disbelief, "You made Death itself pull back. I have never seen anything like it in all my years, and trust me when I say I have seen my share of death." He leaned forward, surrounded by a cloud of pipe smoke. His eyes gleamed intently. "What did you say to Death?"

"Um," Chip said as he scratched his head. "Let's see." Xander held his breath, slowly going purple. "Hmmm. Oh, wait." The orphan paused, and the wizard decided he had to breathe.

"Geez, boy, what is it?" he asked in exasperation.

"No," Chip said. The wizard waited for more. When nothing came, he kept his voice level and tried to smile.

"No, what?" Xander asked again.

"Just 'no,' Chip answered as if it was obvious. The wizard adjusted his blue robes, trying to remain calm.

"So you are telling me you looked at Death and told him 'no'?" he asked, looking at his nails, pretending it was not a big deal.

"Yes." Chip nodded sympathetically as a parent would to a small child who finally grasped a simple concept. The wizard scowled.

"Can you elaborate?" the old man asked, trying to keep the edge out of his voice. When Chip gave him a perplexed look, he reiterated. "Can you explain that in a little more detail, please?" Xander tried to smile but failed.

"Oh, sure," Chip said, giggling, "I said 'no' to Death because I did not want to go with him anymore. At first, I did not care, but then I changed my mind. When you sent me all those memories of your life, I realized I wanted to see all those wonderful places. I wanted to go on adventures. I saw Auntie Clare and remembered how much I loved her. I promised myself I would not give up again. I gave my word. The weapons master says your word is everything. I was also mad that Death was pulling my leg, so the no also told him to let go," Chip added, and grinned. "I don't know about my eyes changing colour, but I knew he would listen. I felt really powerful. After, I saw the Wall thing again, but then it disappeared."

"I see," the wizard said in an even tone. "And how did you know Death would listen?"

Chip shrugged. "I just did. I knew talking back to Death would surprise him enough that I could get away. I made him really mad though."

"No doubt," Xander laughed and slapped his knee. "Well, you are an interesting boy, Chip. I think it prudent to keep an eye on you. Let me know if you see or remember anything else." He got up and stretched. "Time for bed, I am afraid. I have had a long journey."

"Where did you go?" Chip asked.

The wizard paused, scrutinizing the boy for several moments. "That is for another time," he said softly.

Chip watched the old man leave, feeling happy that a great wizard had taken an interest in him, even though he was not sure why. As time passed, Xander would acknowledge him when he came to the yard to talk with the weapons master. Sometimes, the boy would feel like they were talking about him because they occasionally glanced his way, but he knew that was a silly thought. There were much more important things for a wizard to do than worry about an orphan.

3

"Self-discipline is freedom."

The weapons master allowed the boy to wrestle with the meaning.

Chip was about to disagree with the statement but realized he had been looking at it wrong. Those who have no self-control cannot be free. They are slaves to any vices that control them. True freedom can only be achieved with discipline. A thought came to him.

"What about bad people?" he asked. "If they have discipline, does that mean they are free?"

"Good question. People who are slaves to their addictions are not free. An evil man is usually chained to his lust for power. He may be disciplined in many ways, but he is a slave to his desire for all forms of power and, therefore, not free. Once you understand this concept, you will see what is trying to control you in your own life. Some things are easy to tame, while others must be avoided at all costs. Admitting no control over something is the highest form of self-discipline. Be gentle with yourself and others, and be forgiving, for self-discipline is a constant quest. However, it is much easier to achieve if you understand the end goal is freedom." The boy nodded, letting the words sink in.

Time passed, and the orphan learned many new skills and habits. Garth Stone upheld his promise to the king by training him harder than anyone else. After school, the boy would also partake in the soldiers' afternoon training sessions. Following that, he had time to eat dinner and do chores before his private evening classes. Though small for his age, Chip developed whip-like reflexes and became adept at other sports.

In Chip's second year of training, he brought his best friend Chase to the weapons master after school one day.

"Can my friend join the afternoon drills with the soldiers?" he asked. They looked at the commander expectantly.

The weapons master seemed about to refuse, but Princess Eleanor had accompanied the boys and chimed in. "He's really fast and strong, high commander. I think he would make a fine soldier one day." Though she was only twelve summers old, the princess already knew how to be persistent enough to get her way.

Garth Stone eyed her suspiciously for a moment, then assessed Chase. "Are you the squire's son?"

"Yes, but that job looks mighty boring, and in all honesty, I don't like the king," Chase said.

Princess Eleanor gasped. "He did not mean that commander. It was a bad joke. He tries to be funny sometimes." Chase looked at her blankly.

Garth arched an eyebrow, and Chip recognized the faintest smile, which would be the equivalent of a full laugh for others.

The High Commander of Vanalon turned to Chase. "Run and climb over those obstacles in the yard." He picked up several items and threw them at the boy. "Catch!"

Chase was fast and displayed natural athleticism, dropping nothing. The weapons master seemed to see his potential. The commander nodded his agreement to the princess.

"Chip could use a sparring partner his size," Garth told the tall boy. "Don't fall behind or get in the way." He dismissed them all with a wave of his hand. The princess looked shocked that someone with a lesser title had dismissed her. The boys hid their smiles as they watched the petite girl lift her finger to scold the high commander. Garth Stone gave her a look, and the authority emanating from him stopped her cold. The princess instead found herself thanking him before departing.

"Now I understand why he commands the whole garrison," she whispered to the boys as they left the yard. Chip nodded, trying not to laugh.

From then on, the orphan's life became a blur of school, training, and private instruction. The boy was so busy that he had almost no time to see Auntie Claire, but she understood. Prince Rupert became more insufferable as time went on. As Chip progressed in physical and academic development, Rupert became increasingly envious. Princess Eleanor was usually enough of a shield between them, but it all came to a head in Chip's third year of training.

After the prince had taunted him mercilessly one morning, Miss Owl sent them outside for their usual break. Chip walked towards the field to get one of the leather balls for a game, when someone pushed him roughly from behind. His training was the only thing stopping him from falling flat on his face.

Instead, the boy rolled into a ball at the last moment and came to his feet, spinning around with his hands raised. Rupert stood surrounded by his usual three sidekicks, pointing at Chip and laughing. His large gut jiggled.

"Next time, move faster, orphan boy," he jeered while his friends snickered. Princess Eleanor immediately intervened.

"Leave him alone! Being a prince does not give you the right to push people. He may be an orphan, but he's more of a man than you are!" she said, fists on her hips. Prince Rupert's laugh cut short. His face turned bright red as he approached his little sister, hands clenched.

"Don't you dare speak to me that way! I'm going to be king someday and be able to exile all the orphans in the kingdom, starting with him!" He pointed at Chip, his hatred clear.

"I will not let you, neither will Mother," she yelled. "You will never be fit to be king anyway. All you care about is being mean and stuffing your fat face!"

Rupert's mouth worked furiously for a moment, but no sound came out. He lurched forward and slapped her hard across the face.

Without thinking, Chip reacted. As Prince Rupert tried to slap her again, the orphan scooped the small girl around the waist and swung her to the side. Chip ducked easily to avoid the next slap and stepped behind the prince with one foot, driving his shoulder into the big boy's belly with all his might. Rupert flailed off balance, his arms windmilling in the air before toppling backwards like a starfish. A look of pain and anger crossed his contorted face.

"Get him!" he screamed at his friends, who were standing open-mouthed. They were lumbering brutes who enjoyed bullying. The three of them turned to Chip and attacked. Rupert's friends were older than the orphan and much bigger but untrained. Chip stepped left as the first boy, Biff, charged him with a wild right hook. He dodged the punch and came back in at an angle. As trained, he was now inside the older boy's guard, and he struck upwards into Biff's chin with full force using the base of his hand. The large boy grunted as his eyes rolled back. Chip followed through with a front kick to Biff's stomach and spun around to the next attacker.

The largest of the group, Chubs, threw several punches at him. Chip blocked a sloppy hook and countered by striking him twice in the face with his fists, drawing blood. He turned in time to duck a vicious swing from another large boy, Gunter, and then grunted as something struck him in the back. It was a sloppy kick from Rupert, who had regained his feet.

Chip advanced on the prince as his anger flared, and he felt two more shots rain down on him from behind. Suddenly, something opened in his mind that he had not felt since his encounter with Death. It was something just out of reach. Instead, he shoved it aside and found the Calm, as instructed by the weapons master. He could hear Garth's voice in his head as he applied the technique, 'Calmness is mastery.'

The Calm was a mental state that soothed Chip by shoving out all thoughts and allowing the boy to react to his current environment as trained. He had spent months refining it to the point that he could usually summon the powerful technique at will. The Calm eliminated all emotion, including fear, and let the habits take over.

Chip felt another fist graze the top of his head, with several more coming towards him. He leapt to the side and landed a full-force turning kick into Gunter's sizable stomach. Spinning around, he planted two more punches to Chubs's already bloody face.

Suddenly, somebody pulled him from behind. It was Chase, flailing like a maniac. He had grown larger than Chip over the last couple of years and was equal in size to the older boys. He had also been training with the soldiers. Prince Rupert and his friends held their ground momentarily, but after Chase clobbered Biff to the ground, they broke and ran.

Chip clasped his best friend's hand in gratitude as they laughed at the fleeing bullies.

It didn't take long for Prince Rupert to run back with the guards. "Arrest them!" he screamed, pointing at the boys. "They attacked me and must be punished!"

Princess Eleanor had regained her composure and stood before her friends with tiny feet planted. "Rupert, Chubs, Biff, and Gunter are the ones that should be arrested for attacking us. The boys behind me were coming to my aid." She looked pointedly at her brother, who was starting to show fear at the realization that he may be in trouble too. He did strike the princess in front of many witnesses. "But an apology will suffice if my brother admits he made a terrible mistake."

Prince Rupert paused for a moment as his round face digested the information. Then his expression turned into a sneer. "Do you really think they will believe you or this… demon orphan over me? I'm next in line to the throne. Guards, arrest them!"

The guards looked at each other with obvious discomfort. They knew the commander trained the boys, so they were not about to step on his toes, especially with the princess blocking their way.

Prince Rupert looked at them in disbelief, then ran back towards the palace. He beseeched the king to intervene, and they were all hauled before the royal court.

King Barton, after listening to both sides, cleared his throat. Chip knew by the way he looked at him that the man was going to make a rash judgment. "I believe my son, the Prince of Vanalon, was viciously attacked in an unprovoked manner by this orphan boy who will now be..."

"Excuse me!" Queen Charlotte stood up and glared at the king, who looked at her wide-eyed, shrinking in his chair. "Our son dared to raise his hand to our daughter, the Princess of Vanalon, and you wish to punish someone who came to her aid?"

The queen rarely worked herself into a rage, so the king, after taking one look at his shaking wife, allowed the irate woman to handle the affair. He excused himself from the court, citing a 'stomach disturbance.'

The queen chastised Rupert and, as punishment, had everyone, including the prince and princess, clean the stables for a week.

After that, they all made an uneasy truce.

As Chip's sixteenth summer approached, he grew taller, though still slight for his age. The boy was slender but finally developing muscle upon his growing frame. According to the princess, he was handsome, but to himself, he looked plain. Chase was already well-muscled and ready for his Manhood Quest, which the teenager would take first, as he was two weeks older than his best friend.

Eleanor, a little older than both, had blossomed into a beautiful petite princess with long, flowing chestnut hair. Her castle duties were increasingly pulling her away from the other two, but they still got together when they could and devised all manner of mischief. The friends all felt an inseparable bond with each other that they knew would continue regardless of which path each took.

Chase completed his Manhood Quest at the end of summer, but according to the Oath of Secrecy, he could not share the details. He did wink at Chip, saying it was quite the experience.

At sixteen years of age, every boy had to take the test. It was a two-day journey to the Pass of Death, where each would gaze solemnly at the barrier and make an oath to the kingdom of Vanalon to defend all humankind. If the barrier was ever breached, Vanalon needed to warn the rest of humanity. As the westernmost kingdom in the land of Amrika, it was their sole duty. Fortunately, nothing had entered the pass for three thousand years, give or take.

Autumn finally arrived, and it was Chip's turn to embark on his Manhood Quest.

Standing on the valley rim, the boy brushed a shock of brown hair from his green eyes and shook himself from his reverie. He set aside his childhood memories to focus on the present. To complete this journey, he needed to follow the weapons master's teaching and live in the moment.

The orphan gave the kingdom of Vanalon one final nod before turning around, squaring his shoulders, and setting off towards the giant peaks.

It had taken all morning to get to the rim of the valley. That was the easy part. He was now entering the dangerous leg of his quest. It would take him the remainder of the day to get to the base of the two massive mountains that rose before him, forming the fabled Pass of Death.

He would stay overnight at base camp and then make the climb to the isolated sentry watchtower at the top the next day. The boy would take his oath while facing the lands beyond, spend the night at the post, and then proceed home as a defender of humankind. He grinned at the thought of such an achievement, given his background.

Chip knew that if he completed his quest, the kingdom would have its Autumn Harvest Ceremony in a month's time, whereupon the king would announce his station in life. Chase would receive his pronouncement at the same time. Given their training, he prayed King Barton would make them soldiers. However, depending on the mood of the king, the orphan could be destined for a life of servitude and subservient chores until the end of his days. He controlled the sudden feeling of panic that swept over him at the thought. Chip immediately found the Calm in his mind that Garth Stone had instructed him to seek when stressed. After years of practice, he could do it easily.

The boy shook his head, marvelling at what he had learned under the tutelage of the weapons master. He felt excited to apply the truths he had internalized to his Manhood Quest.

Chip grasped the hilt of his sword in reassurance as he gazed across the uneven terrain. This was wild country. Giant foxes, bears, and razor-toothed boars prowled this area, though usually they did not venture this low. The apex predator, the huge mountain wolf, was king of the Grey Mountains. Most villagers rarely glimpsed one, as they were cunning and preferred to keep their distance from humans.

Of late, however, there was talk in the surrounding villages of darker creatures that screamed in the night, all teeth and claws. Of course, the villagers always told high tales to scare the young into obedience, but this time was different. Several folks had gone missing in the last couple of weeks, to the point where the king had to send out scouting parties to pacify the people.

Recently, one party had found something so torn apart and dismembered that it was unimaginable to think it could have been human. Upon return, the soldiers were white-faced and closed-mouthed about what they had seen. The men had consulted in private with the commander, who returned with a grim expression.

Garth Stone met Chip the morning of his departure and warned him to be on high alert once he left the safety of the valley. The boy knew to heed the warning. The weapons master was not one to make up stories or spread rumours.

Ahead of the orphan was a deep pine forest.

The safe valley rim had been the boundary he had never crossed. Although countless boys had completed the quest before him and reached manhood unscathed, some did not make it. A few disappeared, never heard from again. Being a solo quest, there were rarely any witnesses to what befell the missing boys, though sometimes the evidence of a struggle indicated which creature had borne the child away.

Traditionally, the quest was considered fairly safe, but these were different times. He would heed the weapons master and take the utmost care.

Chip entered the forest with senses alert. The pine trees were in long rows that seemed to go on forever. He moved carefully between them along a faint trail. The light dimmed into a deepening gloom as the thick branches blotted out the afternoon sun. The boy could hear the buzzing of insects as he breathed in the fetid smell of decaying growth mixed with the vigorous green pine scent that spoke of high mountains and untamed rivers.

He permitted himself a wide grin. For the first time in a long while, he felt free. The boy had slept for years in the cramped quarters of the storage room and stable. Every chance he got to go outside, even to train, he jumped at it. They had pushed Chip hard his whole life, and he tried to never complain. He knew that as an orphan, they owed him nothing. Every day, he was grateful for having a place to live and a chance to learn something. But, after six long years of school and training, the boy was ready for a change. He shook his head ruefully. Things were about to change; he just knew it.

As if on cue, something dark flashed across the trees to his left, at the edge of his vision. All thoughts of castle life vanished, and Chip froze behind a thick pine. Ever so slowly, he peered around the trunk. Only trees met his gaze. It was possible he had imagined it, but Garth always told him to trust his senses.

Something was with him in the forest.

He broke from the tree and darted forward with light footfalls to put as much distance as possible between himself and the shadow. He heard a twig snap faintly behind him to the left. When he whirled around, nothing was there. The forest, though, had gone eerily quiet.

He increased his pace to a light run, avoiding roots and holes. He also veered diagonally. A branch broke behind him, much closer now and then another. He caught a glimpse of something large and black between the trees.

Chip's heartbeat quickened as he unleashed into a full run, dodging trunks and ducking under bushy branches.

A loud, bloodcurdling roar exploded behind him, shattering the silence. Something monstrous crashed through the brush, closing fast. His panic threatened to overwhelm him, but the boy refrained from turning around, which would cost precious moments he might need. His inner voice screamed for him to focus. Chip knew his life was in imminent danger and felt the suffocating power of fear. All the countless hours of training flashed before him.

Focus! he thought.

Whatever was behind the boy was large and fast, closing the distance rapidly. He concentrated hard and managed to find the Calm in his mind. For a moment, he was in a sea of serenity surrounded by a hurricane force. His focus crystallized as he looked right and left.

There!

A large pine tree stood to his left with its lowest branches about seven feet from the ground. The black thing was now right behind him, thrashing wildly. Chip careened towards the tree, running full speed, and leapt at the lowest branch. He managed to catch the limb with both hands and then, with all the force he could muster, swung his knees up.

Something caught the back of his cloak as it rushed by, shredding it as he scrambled up. Without even looking, Chip jumped onto a higher branch as a monstrous clawed hand tore into the tree limb he'd been standing on.

The boy climbed up even higher before looking down. What he saw made his heart skip a beat.

The biggest fanged black bear he had ever heard of was standing on its hind legs, roaring at him just out of reach. It was easily eight feet tall with a massive shaggy body and two one-foot-long fangs jutting like curved scimitars from its immense jaws. The beast bellowed at its prey, and the orphan shrank back from breath that reeked of rotting meat.

Horrified, he watched as the huge bear put its arms around the trunk and started shimmying upwards. Chip turned in panic and clambered frantically up the tree as fast as possible with the sole intent to reach the top. The bear pursued him, closing the distance.

When it got wedged between too many branches, the beast savagely struck down on nearby limbs with its monstrous claws, tearing some right off the trunk. The bear was slow but relentless.

Chip was approaching the very top and then stopped. It did not feel right. If he was stuck at the top, where would he go? The bear would simply shake him down or even smash the top until he fell right onto it. He made a bold decision and jumped back down to the advancing bear. It roared with anticipation, sensing its prey within reach, bloodshot eyes almost bursting from its massive head.

The limb Chip landed on was directly above the bear and extended outward. He believed it would hold his weight while leaping to the neighbouring tree. Giving one final look at the bear, he ran across the limb even as it tried to swipe at him. Before the end, he pushed off hard. Chip clenched his jaw as he jumped, praying he would not hear the one thing he dreaded most.

Crack!

The branch partially broke as he pushed off. Chip sailed through the air but missed his intended target. At this height, the boy knew he would not survive if he hit the ground. In a panic, he reached out and fell through the ends of two branches in the neighbouring tree, grasping in desperation for anything to hang on to. He managed to clutch a third lower branch, which broke as well.

The orphan grunted as he landed on an even lower branch, then scrambled across it until he could hold the trunk, gasping with relief. The bear let out a snarl as it saw its prey escape to an adjacent tree. Immediately, the beast began shimmying down.

Chip gulped and jumped across the lower branch to the next tree and luckily found another broad limb that led to the tree after that. In moments, he had put a good distance between himself and the bear.

As the beast neared the ground by the first tree, Chip needed to decide if he should make a break for it or stay in the trees. The boy was about to jump down and run for it when the forest went completely silent. Even the bear, which had now landed on the ground, stopped moving.

Nothing happened until the bear lifted its giant, shaggy head to sniff the air. Chip silently lowered himself to the ground and peered around the trunk. What he saw made his blood run cold.

A dark thing on two legs was approaching the bear from behind. Sensing a presence, the fanged black bear whirled around on its hind legs and emitted a deafening roar. The figure calmly circled the bear, finally coming into full view. Chip stifled a gasp.

The creature was from a nightmare. Its naked form was manlike, but the elongated muscled arms ended in long, sharp claws that reached its knees. The thing's face was flat, containing a huge mouth bristling with large, razor-sharp teeth. The eyes were almond-shaped and completely black with no whites. Tufts of long hair covered parts of its naked, dark grey body. The creature moved smoothly, muscles rippling, and crouched in front of the bear.

Bellowing, the black bear stood up on its hind legs to prove its superiority and then charged at the creature, swiping mightily with its front claws. Nothing could withstand such brute force, yet the creature ducked in a blur of motion and appeared at the side of the bear. It struck down with two windmill motions of its claws at the bear's shoulder, cutting straight to the bone.

After the second swipe, the bear's arm came off cleanly. A burst of blood sprayed out from the amputated limb. The black bear roared in pain and snapped at the figure with its great jaws. Displaying incredible speed, the creature dropped below the massive fangs and disembowelled the bear with two arcing sideswipes of its razor-sharp talons.

The bear's intestines spilled out onto the forest floor in a steaming pile. It dropped to its knees and began to fall forward. The creature stood upright in front of the falling bear and grabbed its massive shaggy head on either side. It gazed into the animal's dying eyes, then opened its mouth wide and bit deep into the flesh of the bear's neck. The thing latched on, drinking greedily from the wound. The bear shivered and then went still.

Chip watched in disbelief, remaining motionless. After a long feed, the creature let the bear fall sideways, and the body slumped to the ground. Everything was quiet. Chip stood frozen, trying to calm his thoughts. As if reading his mind, the creature slowly turned around.

The boy moved behind the trunk without making a sound. For several agonizing heartbeats, nothing happened.

Chip heard the thing sniff the air and start moving. His worst fears became reality as the sounds of its claws scraping the forest floor grew louder. He dared not make a sound yet knew it was only a matter of moments before it rounded the tree.

The steps moved closer, and now he could clearly hear its raspy breathing. It stopped behind the tree and sniffed the air again.

An excited whine escaped its lips, chilling the boy to the bone.

A deep growl suddenly came from the location of the bear's dead body. Chip heard the clawed creature turn around a few feet from his hiding spot. The boy peeked around the right side of the tree, and his eyes opened wide.

A huge mountain wolf stood over the bear's remains. The great dog growled threateningly, bunching its massive shoulders and baring long teeth. A hungry, inhuman shriek escaped the dark creature on the other side of the tree, and it ran back with frightening speed towards the monstrous wolf. The huge dog lowered its great head and crouched down on all fours, almost allowing its belly to touch the ground. Its tensed muscles formed thick ridges along the grey and silver fur.

At the last moment, the clawed creature leapt high in the air to land on the immense animal. As it came down, the wolf unleashed its taut muscles like a spring and shot straight up, a blur of dark motion. Its massive canine jaws fastened around the creature's neck, twisting at the same time.

There was an audible crack as the thing's spine broke, and it went limp immediately. The mountain wolf landed heavily with the creature still in its jaws, throwing it sideways and shaking its great head as if to rid itself of a foul taste.

As the giant dog began to look up, Chip hid again, praying it would not come his way. The boy controlled his breathing, still processing what had unfolded. He heard the wolf pad across the forest floor, but thankfully, the sound was diminishing. He risked a quick peek around the trunk and saw the great beast disappear into the far trees. When the mountain wolf was out of sight, he cautiously waited a little longer. The sounds of the forest began to resume.

The orphan released his breath and immediately took off at a low run across the earthen floor. After a short while, he reached the other side of the forest and saw the two great peaks of the Pass of Death in the distance. He sighed in relief and continued onwards without stopping, grateful to put the forest behind him.

The boy's relief was fleeting, though, as he could not shake a foreboding sense that there might be more of those dark creatures with him in the mountains.

Chip knew he would have to hurry to reach base camp before nightfall.

4

The land had changed to rocky patches with low bushes, all leading down to the mighty Rocky River. From there it was an uphill climb to the base of the peaks. The boy alternated between walking at a brisk pace and a light run. He continued downward, taking cover where he could, constantly scanning the surrounding horizon lest he spot another dark creature.

The villagers had been right. They said something with teeth and claws was roaming the countryside. They did not realize it was powerful enough to defeat a massive, fanged black bear, which was a formidable adversary in this region, second only to the mountain wolf, the apex predator of the Grey Mountains. Even so, he had never heard of a wolf so large. Knowing it was still in the area disturbed him.

The boy glanced down at the sword given to him solemnly for his Manhood Quest, a gift from Garth Stone who said it was awarded to him many years ago when he won the Silver Sword tournament at the Wizard's Guild. He had completed his training as a Protector and entered the contest upon the urging of his fellow graduates. To win, he had to defeat another rising star named Maxim, and then his own Master in the finals. The epic swordfights became the stuff of legend.

Chip had tried to refuse the sword as he had no right to such a gift, but Garth was firm. Besides, when the weapons master became Xander's Protector, the master smith in the Guild forged him a new blade. Chip had accepted the sword in wonder, amazed at how light it was. It was an extremely rare elven blade of the highest quality. Since the elves were likely no more, it had incredible value.

Chip's ears discerned the dull rumble of water. He could see the arc of the river where it began high up in the glaciers on the peaks to his left. With cliffs and high gorges, those mountains were considered impassable. The ones on his right were equally fearsome and avalanche-prone with steep, jagged sides. No one could traverse them save for the hardy mountain goats that inhabited the upper steppes. The only route through to the other side was the pass straight ahead.

With late afternoon approaching, he arrived at the great Rocky River. The sound of the rushing water drowned out everything else. He plodded forward until the bridge came into view and stopped to scan the large wooden structure from end to end. Nothing moved. He cautiously approached the bridge.

Stepping onto the wooden planks, Chip ventured to the middle and looked over at the rushing water below. The dangerous river widened and rushed through a series of rapids and steps before entering the valley in the distance. He turned to scan the land ahead, which began to rise to the peaks where he would stop for the night at base camp. He estimated it to be about another hour's hike.

Chip adjusted his pack in the middle of the bridge and took one last look behind him. His heart skipped a beat. There, standing at the end of the bridge, was another dark creature.

Long, muscular arms ending in long claws were hanging at the ready by its sides. The thing's mouth split in a wide grin as it eyed Chip hungrily. Rows of sharp teeth dripped saliva. A black tongue snaked out to lick thin lips. The monster stood naked with clumps of dark hair covering various parts of its body. The boy shivered in terror but stood firm. He dropped his pack on the ground and drew his sword in one fluid motion.

The blade shimmered in the setting sun.

Chip had trained for six long years with one of the greatest weapons masters in the world. Though he was not full-grown, few men in the Keep could come close to him in skill, aside from Garth and Chase. He was confident in his abilities but shuddered at the speed of this creature. He would welcome a sword fight with any man over this monstrosity in front of him.

The boy looked into the face of the beast. The creature stood with a lecherous grin framing a multitude of sharp teeth. Chip reached across his waist and pulled out a dagger to hold in his left hand. This was not a common thing for him to do as he preferred two hands for his sword, but he felt the dagger would serve as both a weapon and a type of shield against its sharp claws. He was well-versed in both.

Strangely, the roar of the water allowed him to hone in on the Calm. The boy dispelled thoughts of death and fear through deep breaths. He focused on the creature. Part of the Calm mentality was to accept that he might not survive. The weapons master made it clear that only with the acceptance of death can warriors achieve their full potential. If his short life was about to end here, so be it. As that last thought entered his mind, the creature attacked.

It sprang forward, all teeth and claws, emitting a maniacal, frenzied whine. He stood motionless as the distance closed. At the last instant, the thing slashed down at his face with one raking claw while swinging at his midsection with the other.

The speed of the attack was frightening. Chip parried the top claw with his sword and used the dagger to block the other. As soon as he blocked, the creature bent forward with its mouth gaping to bite at his face.

Leaning back cost him power, but it allowed him to avoid the gnashing teeth while sliding his sword down the curve of the creature's outstretched arm. The blade pierced its shoulder at the neck with a deep downward slice. A stream of hot black blood sprayed outward over Chip who leapt back and wiped his eye with his sleeve, which was a mistake. The creature slashed at his exposed belly as it had done with the bear.

Chip only partially parried it with the dagger while using his sword to block its left arm, which now moved slower. He felt a raking talon get through, slicing across his ribs. He moved back to regroup, and the creature paused to lick Chip's blood from its dripping right claw.

The thing's face broke into ecstasy as it savoured the taste, and then the expression turned to one of pure hate. Chip controlled his breathing and ignored the searing pain across his ribs as the beast looked into his eyes.

"Humankind is doomed," it uttered in a voice like dead, rustling leaves. Chip's eyes widened in shock. The creature could speak.

The boy noticed it was having trouble holding up its left arm. The gash between its neck and left shoulder was still oozing thick black blood. He decided to take advantage and danced forward nimbly to slice down with a quick arc of his sword. It swung at him with its other claw, but Chip was ready for it. Parrying the blow with his dagger, he jabbed at the weaker arm several more times, drawing out fresh spurts of blood from up and down the limb. It squealed in pain and shied away, letting its injured arm dangle uselessly.

The creature hissed at him with a menacing glare and stood up as if to provoke him. He remembered the thing doing that once before with the bear. He lunged forward, swinging both blades together as if to pincer it, mimicking the bear's mistake hours before. As predicted, it ducked and moved to his right side in a blur of motion, but this time, in midair, Chip altered his sword's trajectory. He swung the blade back horizontally before its claws could disembowel him. The sword cleanly severed the beast's stomach muscles while he pirouetted to escape any counterattack.

The creature let out a scream as its insides spilled out onto the bridge. It would suffer the same fate as the bear. The beast sank to its knees, not bothering to hold on to its organs. It raised black eyes to him.

"We are cooomiiing..." it intoned in a raspy drawl and swung feebly at him. He parried without effort, stepped in, and decapitated the creature. The head flew several feet across the wooden planks and stopped, features frozen in an evil smile. He shuddered, cleaned his sword, and sheathed the weapon.

The boy surveyed his surroundings, trying to make sense of what had happened. The roar of the water made him feel alive, and he felt a sense of pride at having defeated such a formidable foe. He had been training for so long but had never actually killed anything.

He suspected these beasts were the ones terrorizing the villagers recently and wondered where they had come from. The world was full of strange creatures, but this was a first for the small kingdom of Vanalon. It was possible they had arrived from deeper in the mountains to the north, in territory still unexplored. The higher mountain climate north of Vanalon was largely uninhabitable due to the harsh conditions. The valley and land east were green and luscious, but the surrounding Grey Mountains were perilous.

The city was the last western outpost before the barrier and the ocean beyond. The thought made him look up at the Pass of Death. He realized the sentries posted in the watchtower might have knowledge of the origin of these creatures.

Chip decided to drag the heavy body off the bridge. He considered heaving it in the water but chose to place it beside the structure in case the soldiers wished to analyze it. Carrying the head was particularly disturbing. He washed his hands at the edge of the river, careful not to lean too far in, before taking off his tattered red cloak and black tunic.

He examined the slash across his ribs, which was not deep enough to require sewing. He washed it with the cold river water, then dried and bandaged the wound with a strip of cloth from the undershirt in his pack. Replacing his tunic and torn cloak, he strapped on his sword and pack.

The orphan walked back across the bridge, straight into the setting sun. It was now a dark, fiery orange orb low on the western horizon. The river sparkled as it reflected the last rays of the day. He would struggle to make base camp before nightfall but took a moment to admire the beauty of the land around him. The majestic peaks surrounding the green valley cradled the kingdom as a soothing mother. East of him, far down below, was the One Road leading from Vanalon to the larger city of Calgar and, eventually, the Capital Toron. He turned back to the Pass of Death, anxious to complete his quest. The boy had always longed for adventure and now had found it. Still feeling exhilarated, he permitted himself a broad smile and continued towards the peaks.

The ground began to slope upward towards base camp. The orphan walked at a fast pace, even jogging at times. He traversed flat rock dotted with shrubbery and the occasional copse of pine trees. The air became noticeably colder as the sun began to disappear behind the bottom of the pass.

The boy ran the last league, and by the time he reached the small cabin at base camp, the sun had vanished. The stars appeared in the blackening sky alongside an almost full yellow moon. Chip marvelled at the colour of the celestial body as he inhaled the fresh mountain air, infused with a heady scent of pine.

He approached the dark cabin, scrutinizing his surroundings. Nothing seemed out of place. A ready-made fire stood in a ring of stones before the small wooden structure as a courtesy to the next traveller or those returning from the watchtower. Chip tiptoed up the wooden steps and slowly opened the front door of the cabin. It was black inside. He reached around the doorframe and felt the oil lamp dangling from a chain beside the door. He retrieved it and made his way back to the ring of stones. The boy lit a small bundle of tinder with his flint and steel. He then lit the oil lamp and walked into the cabin, holding it aloft.

There were only two rooms. The first held a large table with six chairs, a log stove with various cooking implements, and a spacious cupboard full of pantry items. The second room held six cots arranged in a row. Every two weeks, a new set of six soldiers stationed themselves in the pass to relieve the previous six. He wondered how much longer the current group had left.

Chip went back to the kitchen and lit the wood in the stove. He dug into his pack and pulled out some bread and hard cheese. These he put to the side and dug deeper until he found a rolled pack of spiced, cured meat, which he dropped in a pot to sear.

Once done, he removed the meat and emptied a small bag of chopped onions, vegetables, and herbs. The fat from the meat made the vegetables cook with a satisfying sizzle. When they softened, he added the meat back with some salted water and let things simmer. Though he hated Miss Stern, he had at least learned how to cook after performing kitchen duties for two years.

Thinking back, he realized how much he missed Auntie Clare. She was still the head midwife, but her hair was almost white now, and she tended to teach and supervise these days. He visited her when he could, but not as often as he wanted.

Life had a way of changing and trying to recapture an experience or a period in the past never seemed to work. In one of Garth's numerous sayings, he advised not to chase the old. It would only lead to disappointment and missing the new. It took a while for Chip to understand what he meant. People grew and changed. The past was gone, or at least that variation of it was gone. The weapons master also said half the beauty of the past was the newness of it, which could only ever be claimed once. The advice, however, did not stop the boy from occasionally yearning to be sitting on Auntie Clare's lap in front of a warm fire while listening to the comforting sound of her voice as she read a story. He would always cherish those memories.

Chip shook himself and took the pot off the stove. Ladling a wooden plate full of rich stew, he dug in, realizing how hungry he was. Pulling off a piece of bread, the boy chewed in contentment and then washed it all down with the cool river water he carried in his wineskin. When he finished, he cleaned up and decided to do a quick scan of the camp to make sure everything was safe.

As he walked the perimeter with his lantern, Chip noticed recent three-toed footprints in the dirt at one side of the cabin that he did not recognize. They were not very large, so he shrugged and moved on. The night sky was now resplendent with bright stars and an even brighter moon, which had risen higher above the horizon.

He breathed in the clean air and decided not to light the outside fire. The creature on the bridge had put him on edge, and an outdoor fire would draw too much attention. Hopefully, the soldiers up in the pass would shed more light on the strange beasts.

He took a final look around and re-entered the cabin. He slid the heavy wooden bar in place to secure the front door and headed straight for the back room. The boy pulled out a blanket and settled down on the cot nearest the door. The warmth from the cooking fire made his eyes heavy, and he realized how exhausted he felt. It was his last thought before he fell into a deep sleep.

A mournful howl shattered the night silence. Chip sat bolt upright in bed, heart beating madly. The lamp in the main room cast a dim glow into the bedroom. His sword was on the floor in its scabbard. A sudden stab of fear ran through him as he sensed he was not alone.

The boy felt a presence approach and turned to see a dark figure arrive next to his bed, so close he could touch it. He recoiled in terror and tried to scramble away, but it was too late. The figure held a small black dagger, which snaked out to slash his throat. His movement made it mostly miss, but the knife still managed to nick his neck. He screamed, swivelled, and kicked out with both feet as hard as he could. The figure flew backwards and slammed into the wall. Chip heard a sickening sound of breaking bones and then watched it slide down the wall, unmoving. Only then did he realize how small it was.

Chip scanned the rest of the room and seized his dagger from his breeches next to the bed. A sword would not be the weapon of choice in these close quarters. He stood in his underclothes and peered out the door, dagger at the ready. Nothing moved in the main room. Chip snatched the oil lamp from the kitchen table and brought it back into the bedroom to see what had attacked him.

The light illuminated a small, dark figure lying motionless at the base of the wall. Two little three-toed feet protruded from the base of its cloak. He crept nearer and moved its black hood aside with the tip of his dagger. Inside was a small, frail creature with a wizened face that looked to have been twisted long ago by evil deeds. Still clutched in its diminutive hand was a small dagger made of black metal. The creature's height could not be more than three feet.

He felt its body with care and knew the impact had smashed most of its frail bones, killing it on the spot. He pried open an eyelid to reveal a black eye with no white, like the creature he had killed on the bridge. The cloak was its only clothing. A thin layer of fur covered its small body. What was it and how did it get in?

Chip returned to the living room and examined the door. The bar was still in place. He looked around the room in puzzlement, then noticed several three-toed prints on the counter below the chimney. It must have slid down the narrow chimney chute with the intent to kill him. The creature was well-designed for such a task, but where had it come from? Also, what had howled in the night?

Chip pulled on his clothes, sheathed his dagger, and pulled out his elven sword. It sparkled in the light of the lamp. The boy pressed his ear against the front door for several long moments, hearing nothing. He lifted the bar and placed it beside the door. Standing to the side, his sword at the ready, Chip carefully opened it and peered out.

It was still dark outside, but dawn was approaching. He leaned out to look left and right. There was nothing visible. The nearest copse of trees was a good distance away. He darted out and walked around the cabin immediately noticing three-toed footprints on the chimney side. This was where the creature had entered. A small woodshed was also on this side, which the creature must have used to get to the roof. He walked to the back of the cabin and stopped in his tracks. There on the ground, embedded in the loose dirt, were enormous paw prints. They could only be from a mountain wolf.

The giant wolves were the only enemy of the Fanged Black bear and rarely came to the valley. Every few years, when one appeared, the villagers would band together and track the beast with torches to drive it out. It preferred remote locations untouched by man where there was mountain game. The wolves were intelligent and extremely dangerous. It must have been the source of the howl that woke him. He was thankful for its timing but terrified that the large beast was in the vicinity. He wondered at the incredible odds of it crossing his path twice unless it was hunting him, of course. The thought frightened him more than the diminutive creature lying dead in the bedroom.

Chip re-entered the cabin and carried the small body outside, placing it in the shed instead of burying the corpse in case the soldiers wanted to examine it. He placed the black dagger in his pack. The gash on his neck was not very deep, yet he had no doubt that if he had remained sleeping, the small dagger would have been more than enough to kill him. He wrapped a strip of cloth around his neck, which stopped further bleeding.

After eating a light breakfast of hard cheese and bread, he set off up the mountain towards the pass. The sun had begun to emerge over the eastern horizon behind him, lighting the two peaks with dazzling brilliance. The air was crisp, and he breathed deeply, marvelling at what had already transpired. What a quest this was turning out to be. He could not wait to tell Chase what had befallen him. Knowing his best friend, the taller boy would scold him for not taking on the mountain wolf. He laughed, thinking of Chase, who seemed unafraid of anything. His friend was keen to test his battle skills against all manner of foes. The weapons master was always reprimanding the eager boy for being too impulsive, yet he was by far the star pupil.

When the commander allowed Chase to train with the soldiers in the afternoons, he displayed an aptitude for fighting. He joined Chip in the private evening sessions soon after. It all worked out, since Chip needed a sparring partner his size. It was in the last couple of years that his friend had grown like a weed, almost reaching Garth's size. It took Chase five full years of training to finally penetrate the weapons master's defences.

Chip remembered them sparring hard, both blurs of motion as they lunged and parried. Their practice swords moved with such grace and speed that onlookers gathered to watch the spectacle. The hardened veteran soldiers nearby were nodding in praise, appreciating the intricacy and artistry demonstrated. They were sparring without restraint when Chase turned unexpectedly as if to spin in an arc but instead flipped his sword backwards. The tall boy used both hands to push it straight into the midsection of the weapons master, who grunted in shock, dropping his own sword.

The gathered crowd froze in stunned silence. Nobody knew what to do. The commander had never lost. Chase himself could not believe it. Garth Stone stood up slowly, holding his ribs, and reached out to place a hand on the boy's shoulder. Chip would never forget the look of pride on the weapons master's face. The crowd then erupted in cheers, and so began the stories of his best friend, Chase Longfellow.

In the year since, Chase's skills had only improved, and he could score more often against the weapons master, though he was still the apprentice. Chip was not quite at their level in skill, but his training still put him well above any soldier in the keep. He was small for his age but learned through sparring how to handle himself against a larger opponent. What he lost in size, he could make up in speed and strategy. In any event, Chase and Garth would be proud of his performance thus far in the quest.

A cold wind blew off the peaks as he continued his trek up the mountain. There was a faint but obvious trail leading up to the pass. The soldiers would traverse the same path as they rotated shifts.

Beyond the pass was the Desolate Plain, which led to a magic barrier erected millennia ago to keep out the so-called demon hordes. Stories abounded about the great wizards and elves of old battling the creatures to save humankind. In the end, they drove the demons to the western edge of the known world. There, unable to fully defeat them, the wizards created a great magic barrier with the use of the fabled Orb of Power.

As the story went, the Orb originally was in the possession of the Demon King, who was about to use it to wipe out humankind in the Great Battle. On the eve of that battle, the Orb was cleverly stolen by a young wizard, who turned the tide of the war. The Demon King had such power though that even with the might of the Orb, the wizards could only contain, not destroy him. The kingdom of Vanalon was created in the valley to guard against their return.

This was what they taught him and the other children in school. Many did not believe it. This all supposedly happened over three thousand years ago. He knew most soldiers believed guarding the pass was ceremonial in nature, an easy job vastly preferable to being on the front lines fighting the trolls north of Toron.

The older veterans who arrived from those fronts were usually missing an eye or covered in scars. They talked of the trolls as monstrous, brutish creatures with skin like tree bark and hands that could rend a man limb from limb. For them, Vanalon was a quiet, peaceful place where nothing happened or could happen. It was an easy retirement. The veterans usually stashed a few flasks of ale in their packs and headed up to the watchtower to tell old stories with their mates or show some young lads the fighting basics. Chip hoped that one day soon, he would be a soldier who guarded the Pass of Death as others had for thousands of years.

The boy stopped at midday to have a cold meal on the slopes. It consisted of some leftover cured meats along with a handful of dried fruit. He was approximately halfway to the watchtower, which he could make out at the tip of the horizon. Chip would get there before dusk, solemnly declare that he was completing his Manhood Quest to the men stationed there, then face the barrier and make the oath to guard the kingdom. All males of Vanalon gave their oath, even though most did not become soldiers. It was a rite of passage to manhood and bound the men of the tiny kingdom to its mandate.

He finished his lunch, shouldered his pack, and continued climbing up the trail. The sun at its apex was warm on his face despite the cool winds. He felt invigorated and happy. Being alone with nature was freeing for someone like him. The stigma of being an orphan had been tough to bear throughout his life. Some still thought he was a red-eyed demon in disguise. He had mostly subdued those fears over the years through his connection to the commander and his dedication to training. The boy had earned a grudging respect from the other soldiers and his classmates. Though

Prince Rupert would never like him, he'd at least kept his looks and comments to a minimum ever since the orphan stood up to him.

Now, Chip only wanted to complete his quest and be named a soldier at the Autumn Harvest Ceremony.

All afternoon he climbed, with the occasional break to glance backwards and stare at the majesty of the valley. Huge mountain hawks glided overhead, sometimes letting out piercing, haunting screams. The kingdom looked like a tiny dot nestled in the small green valley from this height. The pine forest the bear had died in also looked small from this altitude. He could still follow the clear blue line of the Rocky River snaking down from the mountains into the valley below to supply the kingdom with clean, fresh water.

The afternoon sun was dropping in front of him as he continued walking west to the pass above. It was awe-inspiring to see the great orange orb directly in his path as it fell perfectly between the two massive peaks. The watchtower was now fully visible, and he looked forward to resting after an all-day climb.

When he finally reached the great structure, the sun was beginning to disappear between the peaks. Made of rough-hewn full-sized trees, the watchtower rose high in the sky, supporting a large, roofed room at the top. Stairs wound their way up the tower, entering a hole in the floor.

As he crested the top of the pass, the orphan could not resist gazing west for the first time at the Desolate Plain far below. His breath caught in his throat. Chip had never seen such vast emptiness. Nothing seemed to grow on the sandy, rocky floor as far as the eye could see, and then there was simply a white wall. He did not know how else to describe it. The plain seemed to end at a massive white wall that looked eerily as if it was made of smoke or clouds. It stretched across the horizon as far as the eye could see. Lightning crackled within the white mass. The sun itself was disappearing over the horizon of the wall. The barrier was real, after all.

The thought made him laugh as he turned to look around the small camp. There was a large log cabin fifty paces to his left and a small trail leading down to the Desolate Plain. It seemed to end after a few hundred feet. There was no reason to venture down there, he surmised. Chip was unsure what would happen if someone tried to walk into the barrier.

Next to the cabin, a giant, towering pile of wood stood to the side, and further down he noticed another structure that looked like a storage shed. Its door was partially open and hanging at an unnatural angle, which seemed odd.

Where were the soldiers guarding the pass?

5

First and foremost, Chip decided to introduce himself to the men guarding the pass. Looking up, he saw the face of a sentry high up in the open window of the watchtower, gazing over the Desolate Plain. The only way the soldier could see him was if he looked straight down.

Instead of calling up, Chip began to mount the stairs. Taking them two at a time, he felt excited to reach the top. Holding the railing, he walked up through a dark rectangular hole in the floor of the watchtower and emerged into a great circular room with a wide view of the Desolate Plain. Chip opened his mouth to announce his arrival, but no sound came out. He froze in shock.

There were bodies everywhere. Rather, pieces of bodies. Chip nearly fell down the hole as he stepped back. A stench of blood and rot filled his nose, causing him to gag. He yanked his sword out and crouched down, looking for an enemy. Where was the guard he had seen from below?

He then saw a severed head resting on the sill of the giant window overlooking the Desolate Plain. It was a soldier whose vacant eyes would never see again. Scattered around the rest of the room were pieces of human bodies shredded beyond recognition. There was blood everywhere.

The desolate howl of the wind coming off the plain was the only sound. He walked around overturned tables and looked behind cupboards, satisfying himself that he was alone in the large room. It seemed whatever had done this was gone. He looked down the hole at the stairs below to make sure nothing was coming up. Chip determined that even though there were body parts everywhere, only three soldiers were dead in the watchtower. Where were the other three?

After several heart-fluttering moments, the boy decided to climb down and investigate the log cabin. With sword in hand and senses on high alert, Chip descended the stairs in the deepening gloom. The sun had almost disappeared behind the great barrier across the Desolate Plain to the west.

Nothing moved as he reached the ground and crossed the empty expanse to the cabin. Everything was eerily quiet. It all felt wrong. He did not realize it before but the door to the cabin was ajar. It was getting so dark that he knew he would not be able to see clearly inside.

Chip slid his pack off and quietly rummaged through it until he found a small, wrapped torch. He lit it with flint and steel, then held it aloft. With his other hand, he gripped his sword tightly. The door squeaked as he pushed it slowly open and slid through. He gritted his teeth at the sound.

Moving forward, he entered a long room with a large oak table and a set of wooden chairs at the other end surrounding an unlit hearth. Lying on the table before him was a dead soldier, his throat slashed and large chunks of his body missing. The guard's sword was still clasped in a death grip in his right hand. The man had at least tried to defend himself. The soldier must have heard the other men screaming in the watchtower and likely retreated to the cabin as a last defence.

He passed the table and entered the door to the back room, which was smashed to pieces. Inside, he found the other two men. One had fallen by the door and was missing both arms. Blood had sprayed over the row of six cots in the room. The second body lay crumpled under the first bed. He reached to lift the cot up off the fallen man when something grabbed his ankle.

Chip yelled in fear, almost dropping his torch, then realized it was the soldier on the floor, who was still alive. He moved the cot over and dropped into a crouch beside the man, recognizing him from his training. This was an older soldier finishing his time at the keep after an illustrious career on the front lines, often recounting various battles with the trolls over the years. His name was Arpad.

The old soldier turned to look up at Chip. Half his face was hanging off and deep claw marks ran to the bone. The rest of his body was badly rent, particularly his shoulder and arms. Blood was everywhere. How he was alive was beyond imagining. His hand shook as he grasped and held the boy's ankle.

"Warn the kingdom..." Arpad rattled hoarsely. Each breath looked laboured and made a sickening, wet suction sound.

"Who did this to you?" Chip managed to ask. He held up the man's head, so he did not have to strain. The boy tried to ignore the fresh blood seeping off the veteran's face and running onto his hand from the act of speaking. The soldier's one good eye stared at him.

"The demons are here... Warn the king," Arpad whispered in earnest. "A pack of them came out of the barrier in the night, all teeth and claws..." He shook, and his eye started to close. A streak of cold fear hit Chip. If it was last night, then where did they go? He would have seen them coming down the mountain from the pass if they had left during the day. Which meant they were still here!

"Which night did they attack?" Chip asked, afraid to hear the answer. "Last night?" The old soldier nodded. The boy's heart sank.

"Attacked before... dawn today... Did not see them," he croaked, trying to say more, but nothing coming out. Chip realized in shock that this man had been lying here all day with these grisly wounds. How was he still alive?

"Takes a lot to kill this fool," the grizzled veteran rasped as if reading Chip's thoughts. Incredibly, the old soldier laughed. Wet blood drizzled out of his mouth. "Tell the wizard... They are coming. Barrier... falling... Must hide... Light the..." His voice stopped. There was no more breath to make a sound. Arpad's one eye opened in shock. His lips curled and froze in a slight smile as he died.

Chip gently released his head. The boy's hand trembled as he closed Arpad's remaining eye. He stood up and gazed solemnly at the dead soldier. The orphan whispered a prayer to the Creator and slipped out of the room.

A wave of fear washed over Chip. He knew the demons were still here, but where and how many? The boy heard a sound outside that sounded like a squawk. Perhaps it was a bird. The light was all but gone.

He peered out the door and saw the last rays of the sun disappear behind the barrier. A sinister silence permeated the camp. He scanned the area, looking for any sign of movement. His eyes rested on the huge mound of wood and tinder two stories tall. He had thought it was firewood for the cabin but now realized by its pyramid-like shape that it was actually an enormous unlit fire. The signal fire!

The soldiers guarding the pass should have lit it at the first sign of the demons. They likely never had a chance. If the demons had snuck in during the night and attacked the cabin and watchtower at the same time, it would have been impossible to reach the fire.

Arpad tried to tell him with his dying breath to light the fire. Chip remembered there was a soldier in the keep far down below in the valley whose sole job was to watch for the signal and alert the king. He needed to light the signal fire.

Nothing was more important.

Chip realized that the soldier had said "teeth and claws" before he died, which could only suggest that what had attacked him on the bridge was a demon. Now, at least, he knew what the creature was. It seemed so obvious now, but at the time, his mind could not even grasp that demons truly existed. The tiny creature that tried to kill him at base camp must have also been a demon. He realized in horror that, given the accounts of the villagers, the demons must have been slipping undetected over the pass for days, even weeks. If the demons were organized, then these would be the scouts. They were precursors to the larger group of demons that had come through the barrier the previous night to attack the guards.

He tried to process the enormity of what was happening. For three thousand years, nothing had come out of the barrier. Few even believed the barrier was magical let alone hid an army of demons.

The land of Amrika was filled with odd creatures that inhabited different parts of the country. To him, it was much more likely that the demon on the bridge was a strange creature that had wandered in from the inhospitable areas to the north. Demons were make-believe monsters created by village mothers to discipline their children. He himself had been falsely called a demon because of his red eyes at birth. That, of course, proved nobody even knew what a true demon looked like. They had black eyes, not red.

Well, now he knew.

Chip thought he could hear a faint mewling sound in the distance, making his skin crawl, freezing him in place. Dusk had settled over the pass. The only light was the torch in his hand and the diminishing orange glow of the clouds reflecting the setting sun that had passed below the barrier. The watchtower, with its grisly remains, stood starkly silhouetted against the fading light.

Its failed purpose of watching over humankind was at an end. The lifeless, broken bodies inside showed the true frailty of men. A lonely wind blew over the pass, letting out a long, hopeless wail that died to an uneasy silence. Chip listened for movement. Holding his sputtering torch in one hand and his sword in the other, he slipped out the door and crept towards the signal fire.

It was approximately a hundred feet away. The boy had a horrible thought. If he did not light the signal fire, he would be responsible for the end of humanity. Where could the demons be? Did they go back to the barrier, and if so, why?

As he approached the unlit fire, the storage shed came into view. A wave of fear washed over him when he again saw that the door was open, but fully this time. In the deepening gloom, the entranceway was a dark rectangle that could hide anything. He was now halfway to the pyramid of wood. He was almost there. His eyes darted once more to the storage shed.

This time, something moved in the blackness.

White claws suddenly appeared out of the gloom, followed by a face of pure evil. With an ear-piercing shriek, a creature raced out of the door straight at him. Immediately behind the demon, a dozen or more spilled out in a dark wave. They all opened their mouths in ear-splitting screams that froze his heart and blood. For a moment of unimaginable fear and terror, Chip couldn't move. He desperately sought the Calm in his mind but could not form it.

Almost in a detached way, he noticed the demons were all different shapes and sizes. They ran at him in a frenzy, with looks of unbridled hatred. They still had to traverse a hundred feet up the hill to reach him. The signal fire was closer to him than them. He could not reach the Calm, but he could reach the fire, and he latched on to that thought with all the focus he could muster.

Light the fire!

The boy lunged forward, running full tilt towards the pyramid of wood. The demon horde was closing in horrifyingly fast. He accepted with heartbreaking sadness that this would be the last act of his life. He had been scorned and labelled from birth as a demon. It was ironic that he was about to be killed by the very demons he was accused of being.

With that thought, he let out a maniacal scream and raced the remaining distance to the signal fire. In dismay, he realized the horde was almost upon him. Their speed was incredible.

He was not going to make it in time.

In desperation, Chip threw the sputtering torch in his left hand onto the base of the signal fire, then raised his sword to face the demons. The blade glimmered in the dying light.

The torch flew through the air, almost in slow motion, and then an unlucky gust of wind seemed to extinguish the flame as it landed on the kindling in the base.

The orphan's heart sank as he swung at the first demon leading the others. It was a fast, skinny creature with long, thin claws and bones protruding at odd angles out of its emaciated body. With one clean sweep, he took off its head with the elven blade. The hum of the sword in the deepening gloom gave him some small measure of comfort. He gripped the warm hilt tightly.

The rest of the dozen or so demons were upon him. He barely had time to notice a singular figure behind them all, striding up the hill wearing a long black cloak. Its dark eyes shone with a fierce blackness, and then Chip knew true fear. As they descended upon him, he made a last prayer to the Creator and raised his blade high.

A popping sound erupted behind him, and then a massive flame burst forth from the base of the signal fire. The wood must have been treated to catch, and the roaring flame ignited the whole pyramid with blinding speed. His sword shimmered in reflective light, a bastion of hope against the darkness.

The demons skidded to a halt and howled, desperate to escape the hot flames. It was obvious they were terrified of fire. Chip himself staggered forward as the heat struck his back like a wall. The demons retreated a distance, then ventured back tentatively, hissing with rage. They formed a semi-circle around him.

The boy sighed. This was where he would make his last stand. A sense of relief washed over him that he had at least lit the signal fire. He had warned humankind about the coming onslaught. With that realization, peace settled over him, and he found the Calm.

The elven blade sparkled with reflective orange radiance as the demons drew closer. A short, fat one with a piggish face and large fangs rushed him from the left as a tall serpent-like demon sprang at him from the right.

He stepped sideways and flicked his sword to the right, forcing the serpent demon to leap back, then whipped the blade under his arm and drove it straight through the face of the pig-like creature, cutting its squeal short. He kicked it off his sword with his back foot, bringing the blade around to slice the belly of the snake-like creature as it lunged again. The reptilian demon staggered backwards, failing to hold on to its innards as they spilled out between its claws.

He had little time to savour these small victories, as several more came at him from other directions. He whirled and twisted, parrying and feinting, going through the forms and dances he had practiced every day for six long years. Limbs flew, and squeals of pain rang out as he sliced and diced, but there were too many.

A claw got through his defence and raked a long furrow in his thigh. Then another swiped down his left forearm, drawing a spray of blood. He cried out and stepped back, allowing a small, furtive demon to leap in and bite deeply into his ankle. He struck down, beheading the pesky creature, before staggering back.

Chip missed the lunge of another demon who slashed his ribs to the bone. He sliced back in response, taking off its arm, but the damage was done. Another claw ripped deep into the shoulder of his sword arm. The boy gasped in pain. The rest of the demons closed in hungrily, smelling blood. Their mouths dripped saliva as they went in for the kill. The boy held his blade up weakly.

"Back," commanded a high voice from the darkness.

The demons froze as one. They were so close to Chip that he could touch them, and the smell of their rank bodies was nauseating. Their expressions changed to fear, and they withdrew immediately. As they parted to either side, the figure with the long black cloak revealed himself. Chip felt an icy flash of fear. Power emanated from this being, who looked much more human than demon, yet not.

The thing had long, pointed ears and wavy dark hair framing a disturbingly white face that emphasized the large, almond-shaped black eyes. The lips curled back to reveal small, pointed teeth. He had hands with long nails instead of claws, and the pommel of a black sword jutted from his waist. He wore dark clothes beneath his cloak. The demons were clearly terrified of him.

The being walked forward between the creatures. Even the heavily muscled ones with teeth and claws shrank back in deference as he passed. The cloaked form stopped a short distance in front of Chip and sniffed the air.

"I can smell your fear, boy."

The voice was sharp and cold. Chip shivered despite the heat on his back and tried to ignore the searing pain from his wounds. The flames cast his flickering shadow in front of him. The boy suddenly felt as alone as he had ever been. Surrounded by demons on three sides with fire on the fourth, he knew every direction was death. Blood dripped out of his wounds, and hissed on the hot ground by his feet. The being's eyes gazed longingly at the droplets.

"I will feast on your blood tonight," the thing croaked.

The other demons started mewling in excitement. "I will share, my pets," he purred soothingly.

Chip felt the first flickers of anger replace fear. They were talking about eating him as if he were a farm animal. The orphan raised his sword higher until it shone brightly in the night. A wave of weakness washed over him from the effort, but he held steady. A sneer started to curl the boy's lips.

"Who and what are you?" Chip asked in a steady voice. The boy's anger was mounting. He shoved his fear aside. The being noticed his defiance and let out a sharp laugh.

"You fight well for a human. With full strength, you might even have challenged me." He spoke with icy calm. A smile revealed the pointed teeth. "I am the Dark Elf Narcister, Leader of the First Horde. In human terms, I'm similar to a captain. I am strong but insignificant compared to my Master and the Inner Circle, may we grovel at their leisure. We are the first wave of many. Your kind will all die."

He stepped closer. The demons started moaning in anticipation. Chip readied for the attack. Narcister eyed the sword with hate. "Where did you get the elven blade?" he asked, pausing.

"It was given to me by my teacher," Chip answered truthfully. The Dark Elf considered this, black eyes shining.

"The Light Elves are no more," Narcister spat. "They hide from the world. Their age has ended. Ours has begun. Enough talk, boy, my pets wish to feed."

Chip's rage flared.

Narcister drew his sword, exposing a long blade black as night. Shrieks of excitement erupted from the demons watching. The Dark Elf strode towards him.

Chip's anger suddenly revealed something in his mind that was hidden. With shock, he realized it had always been there. It was a Wall that he had seen only twice before in his short life, once with Miss Stern, and again when he faced Death as a little boy. It had disappeared, but now he saw it clearly and knew it would never vanish again.

The orphan howled in rage, and the Wall shattered, revealing an incredible Power. The Dark Elf screamed and attacked him head-on with a two-handed blow from above. Chip looked at it all as if in slow motion.

"No," the boy said, raising his left hand.

Chip's eyes blazed a ferocious red, and a shield of crimson fire blocked the blow. The black blade struck it and instantly melted. The Dark Elf's face froze in shock as he staggered back, staring at the smoking hilt of his sword. He looked up at his adversary. The orphan filled himself with his Power and felt invincible.

"Who are you?" Narcister screamed in fear. The demons shrieked uncontrollably. The Dark Elf dropped the pommel of his now useless sword and stepped back, eyes suddenly blazing bright green. Chip felt the peculiar crackling of magic. Narcister stepped forward, forming a ball of green fire between his hands, and released it at the boy.

Chip instinctively pointed at it, using his anger as a weapon, and released his Power. Red fire lanced from his fingers, incinerating the ball, and easily passing through it towards the Dark Elf. Narcister fell back, trying to form a shield of magic, but the red fire sliced through it as if it were paper, exploding into his chest and sending the demon captain hurtling backwards in a ball of red flame. The Dark Elf screamed once, then landed in a dead, smouldering husk thirty feet away.

The demons wailed in shock, screamed, and attacked at the same time. Chip turned to incinerate them, but a wave of exhaustion swept over him, so instead, he instinctively shrouded himself in a blanket of red fire. The demons tried to slice and strike at him but shrieked in dismay as the fire burned them, melting their skin.

Another wave of exhaustion struck Chip who wanted to bring his newfound Power to bear, but he had lost so much blood. His shield wavered. The boy briefly saw something black and monstrous hurtle from the sky, landing with a thud near the signal fire. The creatures continued focusing on his failing shield, hungrily moving closer. Chip felt his control over the Power slipping.

Then, from out of nowhere, blue fire erupted into the demons. They screamed and turned. Chip looked up in tired disbelief. Incredibly, striding towards him was Xander, arms raised and blue robes billowing. The old man's face looked terrifying as his eyes blazed bright blue. For the first time, Chip saw the true power emanating from the wizard. Gone were the silly faces and sly winks he used when bantering with others. Instead, this was the man from legends, serious and lethal, handing out death at will. Blue fire lanced from his fingers, striking several demons at once.

Behind him, the weapons master Garth Stone appeared, leaping off the black thing that landed from the sky. Chip realized it was a giant bird. Garth landed on his feet and rolled into the frenzied demons. In the roll, he pulled his sword and dagger at the same time, becoming a blur of motion.

Chip's control over the shield was almost gone, and only a small flicker of red remained. He tried to stand straight but felt an enormous heaviness. The boy looked down and saw he crouched in a large puddle of his own blood. Fear struck him, and his shield finally disappeared. The orphan felt helpless.

Garth was a whirlwind of death, slicing off limbs and stabbing black hearts with frightening speed. Chip managed to marvel at the weapons master in his unbridled glory. Nothing was held back as he danced the forms and executed his patterns with perfection. His face looked to be carved from granite.

The wizard wrapped another demon in blue fire, who screamed and ran off into the night before succumbing to the flames. A final lone demon saw the boy's vulnerability and ran at him to rip out his throat.

Chip reached for his Power, but the Wall was back up. "No," he cried weakly and tried to raise his sword. It was too heavy, and his torn shoulder would not respond. The demon leapt on him and opened its mouth to sink its fangs into his exposed neck. As its teeth pierced his skin, he heard and felt a dull thud. Something sharp pierced the boy's chest. The demon's mouth froze on his neck, barely entering his skin. Its mouth would never close.

Protruding from the beast's back was the sword of the weapons master, who had hurled it from several steps away at this last demon. The tip of the sword had passed through the creature into the boy's chest. The demon fell backwards off Chip, taking the blade with it. The wound, thankfully, was not deep. The throw had saved his life.

"Sorry about that," Garth apologized, walking up. "I am afraid it was the only option. Are you hurt, boy?" Chip tried to shake his head from side to side but instead collapsed on his back, dropping his sword.

"Maybe a little," he groaned. Pain and weariness engulfed him. The weapons master crouched down by his side, assessing his wounds, and looked gravely at the wizard. Then Xander was there, concern and wonder etched on his face. He dropped to a knee and placed a hand on Chip's forehead.

"Bring him inside the cabin," the wizard ordered. "There is little time. He has spent much blood."

Garth lifted the boy easily. Chip's head lolled to the side, and he caught a final glimpse of the clearing littered with dead demons. The signal fire shone brightly and filled his entire vision. Yet even that bright light started to dim until he finally fell into blackness.

6

The boy woke to bright sunlight streaming through a window. He had no idea where he was. A door opened, and a figure stepped through. He started to sit up and felt a wave of soreness rush through him.

"Ah, there you are, my boy. How do you feel?" asked the figure, who he finally recognized as Xander.

"Sore," he mumbled. The rush of the night's events filled his mind. He lifted the blanket to look at his wounds. "What happened to my cuts?," he asked in surprise. A sudden fear raced through him. "Am I... dead?"

"My goodness!" the wizard exclaimed, doubling over with mirth. "Not yet. However, it was rather close. I healed you with my Power. I managed to close your wounds, but they will throb for a few days. An adept Yellow Level is more suited to healing than me."

He pulled up a chair.

Chip realized he was lying on a cot beside the hearth in the main living room of the cabin. A crackling fire released soothing heat. He looked around and realized the body of the dead soldier on the table was gone.

Following his gaze, Xander commented, "Garth has removed all the bodies and burned them in the signal fire with prayers to the Creator. You slept through the night. It is late morning."

"Are all the demons dead?" asked Chip.

"For now, yes," answered Xander, "but I fear more will be coming, much more." He looked tired, but his eyes were sharp.

"How did you find me?" Chip wondered, vaguely remembering a great black bird.

"I will answer your questions but first recount to me the details of your quest, leaving nothing out." The wizard leaned back and lit his pipe in a smooth motion. He gestured for the boy to begin.

Chip took a moment to gather his thoughts, then relayed everything he had experienced from escaping the bear to the fight on the bridge. He recounted the attempt on his life in the cabin, and his discovery of the dead soldiers in the watchtower. The boy described his confrontation with the Dark Elf, which caused him to finally see the Wall in his mind and break through it to find an incredible Power. He ended with Narcister's threat of the demise of humanity. Xander's eyes widened at points, but he remained silent. When Chip finished, he stared at the boy for a long moment.

"The king is dead."

"Huh?" Chip said.

"King Barton is dead," repeated Xander. Chip felt a mix of different emotions.

"How?"

"The three-toed creature that tried to kill you at base camp was in fact a demon assassin. They are fast, small, and clever. Their size allows them to go almost unnoticed. Two nights ago, one slipped into the king's bedroom and slit his throat. Queen Charlotte did not realize until morning that he was dead. She looked at him in the light and discovered the man lying in a pool of blood. Her screams woke the guards. They sent for me immediately, and I inspected the scene."

The wizard paused, and his eyes had a far-off look.

"A long time ago, a group of elves removed the Walls to their Power, causing their eyes to go black. The demons are the offspring of those Dark Elves, mutated and twisted. They bred the little ones to be assassins. When I found the king, I looked around for evidence of forced entry or some type of struggle. I spoke to the guards and potential witnesses, but nobody noticed anything unusual. This cast the queen as a possible suspect, but I quelled those rumours. I cannot read a person's mind, but I am rather good at deciphering whether someone is telling the truth. The queen is innocent." He blew a small smoke ring, musing on his memories.

"So how did you know it was a demon?" Chip asked.

"Well, that's just it," he said. "It was too perfect. I knew it must be the work of an assassin. I had seen that type of handiwork before, but it was a very long time ago. I decided I needed to verify my suspicions. I ordered Garth to commandeer two swift horses, and we rode up towards the pass yesterday. We saw the remains of the bear next to the clawed creature in the forest. I recognized the demon's body instantly and knew they had breached the barrier. Afterwards, we discovered the black blood on the bridge and the headless demon body beside it.

"Garth and I galloped to base camp where he found the three-toed footprints around the cabin and the body of the assassin that you left in the storage shed. I surmised it was the same assassin who killed the king. The creature was likely on its way back to report the successful assassination to the Dark Elf demon captain. We found the mountain wolf tracks as well. As a fearless predator, it likely hunts demons it sees as foreign invaders, though it is rare to see one this far south. We concluded that you must have survived both attacks on the bridge and the cabin, then hiked up to the pass. We were only a couple of hours behind you, but it was almost dark, and even on horses, we could not reach the pass before nightfall."

Chip suddenly remembered the great black bird.

"Did you fly?" he asked in wonder. A look of amusement flitted across the wizard's face.

"Why, as a matter of fact, we did," Xander continued to Chip's amazement. "I knew there would be more demons about, and since they prefer to attack at night, I felt you were in grave danger. If a demon had made it all the way to the king, then the guards in the pass were likely dead. Some of the foul creatures would have stayed to hold the pass and await the assassin's report. Despite their looks, the demons are organized and have a strict hierarchy. Since I knew we could not make it in time on horses, I used my magic to summon a great Cockadoo from the cliffs north of the barrier. Few even know they exist. Even fewer would ever risk riding one of the unpredictable beasts. Unfortunately, I had no choice."

The wizard rubbed his backside absently.

"The bird took its time to arrive and immediately attacked us for having the nerve to make such a request. It snapped at Garth and bit me in the behind." Xander looked embarrassed and coughed. "I was forced to expend more magic to tame the beast, but finally, we managed to hop on and fly to the pass. I commanded the horses to meet us there. We saw the signal fire light up, which almost made the silly bird crash, but finally I soothed the beast and made it land outside the circle of demons. Before it landed, I saw you shoot red fire at the Dark Elf before trying to shield yourself from the others. I must admit that when I saw that, I nearly fell off the bird. Even after I leapt off the unruly beast, it tried to snap at me."

The wizard sat back scowling.

"Can't trust a bird," he muttered. Sensing Chip's next question he immediately said, "No, we cannot ride the bird back. A Cockadoo does not take well to riders. Besides, the three of us would be too heavy and in all honesty, I need to rest up. It takes a surprising amount of Power to control such a stubborn creature." The boy looked glum.

Xander's face grew grim. "While you were sleeping, I took my horse down to the Desolate Plain to examine the barrier this morning."

The merriment left his eyes as the wizard leaned forward. "They are coming."

"Right now?" Chip asked with a stab of fear.

"No. We are safe for now," Xander reassured. "But not for long. I cast my Power into the barrier to inspect its strength, and there is no doubt. It is failing." He uttered the words with a finality that spoke of impending doom.

"In certain spots, I detected weakness, enough that the Demon King can send scouting parties to slip through the cracks. It must take an enormous amount of Power from his side to hold the rift open long enough, but he is quite capable. I fear he has grown in strength all these years."

Xander's face changed to one of sadness.

"The Wizard's Guild is a mere shadow of its former glory. When we fought the demons three millennia ago, there were great wizards alive with much magic. We were also aided by the Light Elves and the Orb of Power itself…"

He lost focus, drifting into memory. Chip waited patiently for him to resume, but after an interminable pause, the boy finally blurted,

"Where are the wizards now? Where are the Light Elves? What is an Orb of Power? And how is this Demon King still alive?"

The wizard held up his hand. He blew one last smoke ring and stared at the boy's inquisitive face. "Good questions, but now is not the time for answers. We must make haste to prepare the kingdom. I have waited for you to recover, but we cannot linger. More demons will slip through. Soon, the barrier will fall, and the very fate of humankind will be at stake."

The wizard rose and turned to leave.

"Wait," said Chip, struggling to rise. He felt some pain but ignored it. "Let me ask this one question. Am I a wizard?"

Xander stopped and turned back. He locked eyes with the boy. "Yes, I am afraid you are," he whispered and walked away.

Chip watched him disappear through the door. The enormity of the previous day finally hit him. He was a wizard! He could not wait to tell Chase and Princess Eleanor. He needed to ask Xander more questions about the Dark Elves, but he would wait until the time was right. He then remembered the incredible, indescribable feeling of holding the Power.

Out of curiosity, Chip reached into his mind and found the Wall, which was back up. With a wave of irritation, he pushed against it, but it stood firm. He resolved to ask the wizard how he could remove the silly thing. The boy stood up gingerly and stretched. He noticed a dull pain in multiple places, but overall he felt quite good. Chip pulled on his boots and walked out into the bright sunlight.

"There you are," said Garth with a rare smile. "You put on a good show yesterday. You did not forget your training. Even so, I am happy we dropped in at the right time."

Approval was hard to come by with the weapons master, so Chip nodded in appreciation.

"Thanks for your help. I never thought I would use my training to fight demons," he said truthfully.

Garth shrugged. "They all die the same."

Chip laughed. "I suppose they do."

Xander hailed them to the top of the pass. They both hurried over to the wizard. "Do you see anything?"

At first, Chip was about to say no, but then he spotted a tiny group of black figures running full speed in the distance, far out on the Desolate Plain. They were still very far away.

"Do we wait and spill more demon blood?" asked Garth, hand casually resting on his sword pommel. Chip knew it could be unsheathed faster than thought.

"No. That is a large group, and we must conserve our strength. I fear the use of certain magic may have triggered a response." Xander glanced at Garth and a look passed between them. "Besides, preparations must be made in Vanalon. Pack the horses."

They were ready to go shortly afterwards. The wizard mounted the white mare, holding her reins loosely. Garth sat on the brown stallion with Chip behind him. The signal fire was less than half the size of the night before, but still burning strong. Black blood stained the ground over a wide area. Xander turned his horse to look at the Desolate Plain one more time. The weapons master followed suit.

"So ends the old age," the wizard intoned in a loud voice. "The demons seek to avenge their imprisonment and destroy humankind. They want to reclaim who they were before they fell."

Chip had questions but dared not speak. The wizard sat powerful and straight, silhouetted by a clear blue sky. The late morning sun blazed overhead, yet the heat did not reach them. A cold, howling wind sprung up and blew in off the plain. The dark spot of milling demon figures was already slightly closer.

The boy felt an overwhelming wave of terror. How many more would there be when the barrier fell? How could they win? He shivered.

Xander turned in his direction. "They will come, horde after unending horde. When the barrier falls, they will fill the entire Desolate Plain and push eastward into Amrika, numbering too many to count. Leading them will be a king so powerful that weak humans may die just by gazing at him. He is the Unnamed One, king of all demons." The wizard paused. "Let it be known that a new age is upon us. We have yet to see what it will bring."

He unsheathed his sword, which rang clear, and held it high over the pass. Inspired by his declaration, Garth Stone and Chip both drew their swords and raised them in defiance of the enemy.

"I pledge my allegiance to defend humankind," boomed the wizard. His voice rolled like thunder and reverberated through the Pass of Death.

"I pledge my allegiance to defend humankind," shouted the weapons master, his face a piece of stone.

"I pledge my allegiance to defend humankind," screamed Chip, holding the elven blade high. A jolt of shock swept through him as the boy realized he had completed his quest. Far down below in the Desolate Plain, he thought he could hear the shrieks of the demons in response.

"Make haste," Xander warned, turning and galloping down the mountain towards the safety of the green valley far below. Garth kicked his horse, and the stallion sprang into action, keeping stride.

The small party rode at a brisk pace and reached base camp by mid-afternoon. The sky had begun to cloud over, and behind them in the west, a dark storm was gathering. They dismounted to give their steeds a much-needed rest. The horses could triple the speed of a man on foot, but they needed breaks. If the companions left after a short rest, they could reach the valley rim by late afternoon and arrive in the kingdom by early evening.

Garth took the horses to the meandering brook behind the cabin to drink. It was one of the runoff streams from the glaciers high above. They filled their water skins with clean water and drank deeply. The weapons master pulled some dried meat and bread from his pack to share with the others. As they sat around the unlit campfire to eat, Chip used the opportunity to talk to the wizard.

"Is Queen Charlotte in command of the kingdom now?" Chip bit into a piece of meat, and realized how hungry he was. He was starting to feel like his old self again as his wounds muted to a dull throb.

"No, Rupert is of age and is now king of Vanalon," the wizard said, shaking his head. Chip stopped chewing in shock. "He is a poor choice, especially in this time of need, but I have dealt with inept kings before. Barton was an overweight fool, but generally harmless. If I had my way, Queen Charlotte would sit on the throne. She has always been the voice of reason and was usually able to keep her husband in check. Rupert is young, entitled and needs to grow up fast. In peaceful times, the decisions of a poor king have little consequence. In desperate times, they are vital to survival. I will not suffer his incompetence long even if he were the High King of Toron himself."

"Will Vanalon survive the demon attack?" Chip asked.

The wizard looked at him with great sadness in his eyes.

"I am afraid Vanalon is lost. All we can do is hold off the demons long enough for the other cities to prepare. We need time to find the one thing that has a chance of stopping them." He looked off into the distance. "Even that I fear will not be enough. The Demon King has had three millennia to nurse his hatred and grow stronger. The great wizards of old are gone. The Light Elves have vanished. We are but few.

"Yet, life has always been about balance. The Creator provides a means for us to survive. We must believe that." He studied the boy. "Perhaps you can help us turn the tide."

"I will try," Chip promised. But how much difference could he really make, even with his newfound magic? "How come my eyes go red when I use magic?" he asked abruptly.

The wizard coughed and hid his face. Even Garth looked startled for a moment. Xander began mumbling as if debating with himself. Chip looked around in confusion then focused on chewing. He looked up sneakily after a bite and saw the wizard studying him. Xander then glanced at his Protector, who nodded. The old man sighed.

"Very well. You are not ready, but time has forced my hand. Then again, are we ever really ready? I will tell you what I can tonight once we reach safety in Vanalon. For now, you must remember not to speak to anyone of your Power. Not even to Chase or Eleanor. Do you understand?" The boy was going to object, but nodded sullenly. The wizard continued, "We killed all the demons in the pass, but such an expenditure of magic can be felt by experienced users. All magic wielders can sense magic, not just see it, but some are more attuned than others, especially the more powerful ones. It is unlikely that the use of your magic could be felt through the barrier, but the Unnamed One's powers cannot be underestimated. I fear the horde of demons we saw running on the Desolate Plain may already be in response to our use of magic. Even so, I am praying that your specific magic was not recognized. If so, all may be lost before it has begun."

Chip looked puzzled.

The wizard acknowledged his confusion and tried to reassure him. "I will explain in due time, but for now, we must keep you safe, and unless it is life or death, you must not use your magic until we are much further away."

Chip almost laughed. "Not sure if I can anyway. There's a Wall blocking it."

Xander looked at him gravely. "That Wall is the greatest protection we have. For now, understand that anger can break through it. Fear will put it back up." His gaze bore into Chip. "If you of all people ever lost your Wall, then may the Creator help us."

For the first time ever, Chip saw a glimmer of fear in the wizard's eyes.

"Grand Wizard," the weapons master interrupted, a rare edge of concern in his voice. Chip had never heard him address Xander like that before. He pointed up the mountain. The demons had crested the pass and were bearing down on them at full speed.

The wizard looked up in alarm, his eyes blazing bright blue.

"They should not have been able to cross the Desolate Plain that fast." Chip felt the peculiar crackling of magic. The old man snorted, "They have handpicked demons built for speed. Hidden in their midst is a strong presence which seems familiar..." Xander's voice took on an edge of urgency. "If they have cut the distance that fast, then we will not be able to return to Vanalon in time. Our best hope is to make for the bridge and make a stand there. They bring a storm with them that looks unnatural." A look of weariness creased his face. "Perhaps I have underestimated their strength. Swiftly then, let us ride."

Garth ran for the horses that were still drinking from the stream behind the cabin. Chip put the rest of the food away. As they mounted, a terrifying distant wail echoed off the high slopes. The demon horde was still a black speck far away, but the eye could discern them moving even from such a great distance. An enormous rumble of thunder broke the air above the pass, underneath a gigantic, billowing black cloud.

Chip felt a stab of fear. Watching him, Xander said,. "Use your magic only if you must. If the Demon King finds out who you are so early..."

The wizard left the thought unfinished as he kicked the flanks of his horse, which vaulted down the trail. Garth did the same. The boy knew the mounts had not rested enough and that their combined weight would slow the stallion down. Chip shivered as he realized an oncoming demon horde was approaching his exposed back. A wind whipped up from out of nowhere, and their horses whinnied in response. More gusts arrived as a harbinger of the storm to come. Chip was thankful that the wizard and the weapons master were both expert horse handlers. They guided their mounts with precision down the trail despite the inclement weather.

About halfway to the bridge, the wind picked up further, buffeting them mercilessly. The horses snorted in protest. Chip could see the green valley of Vanalon far below, but even as he watched, a sudden darkness covered them. Looking up, he saw great black thunderclouds blot out the remaining sun. They did not look natural. A clap of thunder exploded above, causing the horses to panic. Only through years of experience did the riders hold their mounts in check.

No one spoke as time passed. Both men used their full concentration to navigate the winding rocky trail amidst the pounding wind. The boy glanced behind him and recoiled in shock. The demon horde had already reached base camp.

He could almost make out individual figures, their black bodies writhing and twisting. They were covering ground at an insane speed. He looked ahead and saw the great Rocky River below coursing across their path. The bridge still looked tiny from this distance.

The wizard spurred his horse harder as the skies darkened.

The companions pushed their mounts to the point where their mouths foamed. After an intense period of riding, the bridge finally looked within reach. Chip looked back again and gasped. The demons were now only a few leagues behind them bounding down the trail with long muscular limbs. The creatures started shrieking and howling upon seeing their prey within reach. The wind whipped everything into a frenzy. He turned back around, gauging the distance to the upcoming bridge, and with relief believed they would make it in time.

As that thought entered his mind, the sky turned black, and a clap of thunder shook the ground. The air seemed to open as a torrent of rain crashed down on them. The horses, terrified by the sound, broke into a dangerous gallop at full speed. At least they were sprinting for the bridge. Chip hung on for dear life.

They were almost there. The pounding of the wind and rain increased to a terrifying crescendo. At that moment, a jagged bolt of lightning struck a tree to their right. The horses, pushed to their breaking point, careened into each other, and went down.

All three riders flew off their steeds. The wizard grunted as he hit the ground but rolled to his feet. Incredibly, the weapons master swung his leg over as they crashed and landed nimbly in a full run. Chip, unfortunately, did not fare so well. He pushed off the horse as best he could and landed hard on the ground, trying to roll but failing. The air flew out of his lungs, and for several agonizing moments, he could not breathe. As he sucked in life-giving air, someone pulled him to his feet.

"Run, boy," yelled Garth, half-carrying him until he regained his footing. Pain shot through his chest, but he ignored it and focused on the bridge ahead. Xander was nearly there. Chip looked back to see the demon horde almost upon them. Froth covered the creature's faces, and their fangs dripped saliva, but they still ran fast.

The rain fell in torrents as the wind howled around them. The sky was black and angry with lightning streaking across the roiling clouds. If ever there was a moment when he was living in a nightmare, this was it.

Chip ran full speed with all thoughts of pain gone. The bridge was right in front of him. The sound of the rushing Rocky River drowned out some of the storm. Xander had made it to the middle of the bridge and stood with blue eyes blazing. They were almost at the bridge themselves when the demons caught up to them.

The weapons master turned before stepping onto the wooden planks and drew his sword in one motion. Chip pulled his own sword and stopped to stand with him. The demons were over seven feet tall, all teeth and claws. Long and sinewy, they moved with deadly grace. The ones in front jumped the last ten feet with bloodthirsty, gleeful shrieks erupting from fanged mouths. Garth and Chip raised their swords as one and braced for impact.

As the demons sailed through the air an enormous blue ball of fire flew between the two humans and exploded into the horde. The front ones in midair flew backwards in crumpled balls of twisted, fiery limbs. They thrashed and screamed as the blue fire burned them. The others scattered but swiftly regrouped.

"Get behind me," yelled Xander over the rush of the river. They turned and ran to stand behind the wizard. The air crackled with magic. Chip looked at the horde and caught his breath. The scattering of the demons revealed a lone figure standing in the center. A dark brown cloak covered the being from head to toe. The face remained hidden, and strangely the wind and rain did not touch its garments.

The entity strode forward then stood motionless. The demons started closing ranks to attack again. The cloaked figure held up its hand, and as one they slipped sideways to crouch on all fours, awaiting their master's next command. It raised white, human-like hands and brought down its hood.

A pale, handsome face revealed itself. Thin, pointed ears ran into neatly combed hair. A small smile revealed the points of sharp teeth. Unlike the demons, his almond-shaped eyes blazed a bright brown, commanding the elements around him with his Power. The crackling of magic was palpable. He resembled the demon Captain Narcister, but Chip sensed he was much more powerful. The storm howled and raged around everyone but the Dark Elf. He stood in an oasis of calm.

7

"Greetings, Xandrostika. It has been a long time. I have missed you."

The Dark Elf's voice was strong but clear, like a bell, and carried even above the howling wind. Its cadence gave Chip goosebumps. He wondered how the elf could possibly know the wizard. He had been trapped for three thousand years!

Xander spat, "The sentiment is not shared, Elohan. I was rather hoping the Inner Circle had consumed each other by now. This land is not yours. Go back to the darkness from whence you came." The wizard's eyes crackled with blue menace.

Elohan nodded. "I appreciate the request, but I am afraid I have orders from my Master, may we grovel at his leisure, to investigate a… disturbance. An unknown Power was used recently in the pass to hurt my dear brethren. I am simply following up to make sure such disturbances are corrected before they fester into something more. Humankind will fall this time, Xandrostika. It is unavoidable. You wizards are weak, and the Kin are gone. Even the Orb, if found, will not be enough. We have grown strong over the millennia. Your kind will never understand that the Wall in your weak minds is meant to be broken and removed. We will consider a select few who wish to be slaves, but the others will be annihilated once and for all."

He smiled.

"Is that the choice you gave your brother in the Great Battle, Elohan?" Xander asked. The smile vanished. "Does your king reward treachery, even to your own blood?" The Dark Elf's face betrayed his hate.

"He was weak and a fool," screamed Elohan. "He allied himself with the pathetic race of humans. For what?" He visibly controlled himself, contorting his face until it resumed its calm air of superiority. The elf scrutinized Garth Stone and changed the subject. "I see you have a new Protector." He dismissed the weapons master as inconsequential with a flick of his hand. Turning his gaze to Chip, he paused, eyes darting briefly to the elven sword, then asked, "Who is the boy?"

His dark eyes flared a deeper brown and Chip could suddenly feel Elohan's presence enter his mind. For a maniacal moment, he wanted to take down the Wall and push the Dark Elf out with his Power but remembered Xander's admonishment not to reveal his magic. Instead, the boy instinctively surrounded the presence in his mind with the Calm. The Dark Elf's memories revealed themselves, but he seemed unaware of the intrusion. Chip decided to delve into the ones that appeared important. As he did, his sense of time seemed to alter.

He saw Elohan when he was a young elf, noticing he had brown eyes as a youth. Images flashed showing a cruel older elf prince named Killian taking him and others under his wing. Chip gasped inwardly when he saw that the cruel elf had red eyes. Killian showed them the beauty of tearing the Wall down in their minds so they could always feel the Power. It was intoxicating. He revealed the way to take it down permanently. When the practice was discovered, a division arose among the elves.

The cruel elf's eyes eventually turned black, and that night, he murdered his father, King Galal. Killian tried to usurp the throne, but a battle ensued between the elf prince's followers and those loyal to the king. Despite Killian's incredible power, he was significantly outnumbered and suffered a great defeat. The king's younger brother, Luminor, assumed the throne and drove the elf prince west. Killian and his followers fled to the caves in the Fang Mountains. They became known as the Dark Elves and all their eyes turned black. It was the price of permanently removing their Walls. Only when they used Power did their eyes blaze the colour of their Level; otherwise, they remained pitch black.

Centuries passed, and the Dark Elves multiplied, but the unending use of the Power caused their offspring to be deformed. At first, they were horrified but soon realized that the so-called deformities could be strengths. Some of the mutations were far superior to the physical skills of humans. They kept those mutants and formed an army of creatures. The weaker ones were fed to the strong. The mutations varied, but the ones allowed to live grew into terrifying physical monstrosities. The rest of the races named them demons.

Over the millennia, the demon offspring became the norm, and it became increasingly rare for a Dark Elf to be born without mutation. Almost all the demon babies had pure black eyes at birth. The demons could not wield magic themselves and only understood rudimentary commands. It was as if nature allowed them superiority physically but balanced it with diminished mental faculties and the inability to access magic. Any Dark Elf born, in contrast, was always a magic wielder, as all elves were.

Chip put aside his questions and watched as the demons continued to breed and multiply. Some were all teeth and claws, others had pure speed or great strength, and a few were bred diminutively for assassinations. They came in all shapes and sizes, depending upon their mutations. Rarest of all, a demon was born with the Power but could not use it. These were easy to recognize, as they were born with white eyes. If left alone, their eyes would turn black after several months, and they would be indiscernible from their brethren.

One of Elohan's memories showed Killian, now the cruel Dark Elf King, conspiring with a black, hooded figure. They were using dark magic to find a way to draw out the unused Power of these rare, white-eyed demons while they were still babies. The Power transferred to Killian when he ate their remains in a dark ritual, increasing his strength. Occasionally, he fed some to his Inner Circle, but even Elohan found the practice disturbing.

As time passed, the demon army became a fearsome threat. The Dark Elves controlled the foul creatures with their magic. They lived long, unnatural lives due to their continued access to the Power. The elves were already long-lived, but these were almost immortal. For centuries, the Dark Elves clashed with the original Light Elves until their strength became unstoppable. At that point, the race of humans joined with the Light Elves to stop the threat, which sought to overrun Earth.

The cruel elf Prince Killian was now the Demon King, among other names, and grew immensely powerful. He was the only elf born with red eyes. Uttering his name could attract his attention so he was called the Unnamed One by the other races. The Demon King was unmatched in Power, but the combined might of the Wizard's Guild and the Light Elves was greater still. Knowing this, the Unnamed One used his dark arts to search for something that could give him the edge. He found out about a talisman hidden in an ancient city beneath the Earth. It was guarded by powerful magic. Inside the city was an Orb....

Elohan wrenched his presence out of the Calm in Chip's mind. A look of shock and fear passed across his face. "Who are you!" he demanded.

Xander released an immense ball of blue fire from between his hands. It shot across the bridge and enveloped Elohan, who surrounded himself at the last moment with a bright brown roiling cloud of magic. Some fire got through and singed the side of his face. The rest of the blue fire deflected outwards and enveloped several of the demons crouched to the side. They howled and writhed on the ground, skin smoking. Elohan appeared out of the cloud and lifted both arms to the sky. His ravaged, half-melted face twisted with rage.

"Run!" shouted Xander. They started to scramble backwards to the safety of the other side, but it was too late.

A monstrous thunderclap sounded, and the black clouds above opened to shoot a bolt of white-hot lightning down to the middle of the bridge. The wizard's eyes blazed an insane blue, and he threw a thick shield over the three of them.

The lightning bolt hit the middle of the bridge where they were standing moments before with such force that the center burst apart. White lightning energy radiated outward and hit the wizard's blue shield. The wooden planks underneath them disintegrated from the impact. For a moment, they withstood it all, then the shield vanished, and the bridge completely collapsed. They fell headlong into the cold Rocky River.

Chip caught a glimpse of Elohan collapsing from the immense release of energy he had commanded. Several demons who had escaped Xander's fireball leapt into the water after them without hesitation.

The boy went under quickly. He tried not to gasp as the cold water went over his head. It was all he could do to hang on to his sword. Something struck his leg, and he felt his feet hit the bottom. Chip tried to push up, but the force of the river propelled him downwards. He struck something hard with his shoulder and knee, causing him to somersault through the dark current.

The orphan's lungs screamed for air as he forced himself not to breathe. His feet seemed to skim the bottom again, and this time, he pushed with all his might. As he did, the boy's head broke the surface, and he inhaled clean, fresh air.

Chip saw the wizard flailing downstream in his blue robes and the weapons master holding his sword aloft as the river narrowed up ahead. They were about to drop down the first of a series of rocky steps, followed by a waterfall that was not survivable. The mighty Rocky River dwindled into a meandering stream down in the valley, but near the mountains, it was swift and dangerous. The boy paddled valiantly, trying to stay afloat.

A mewling sounded right behind him, causing Chip to turn and see one of the seven-foot-tall demons reaching out to rake his face with its claws. Even the prospect of drowning did not deter the creature from its sole purpose of killing. The boy managed to swim backwards to avoid the thing's elongated black claws, and then the water fell out from under him.

He knew they were descending the first step of the river's descent into the valley. Chip faced skyward as he fell. For over thirty feet, he sailed through the air, looking straight up at the demon descending above him, claws still reaching to tear him apart. It seemed they fell together in slow motion, and his singular focus became the creature.

He could almost reach out and touch it. As if frozen in time, the boy saw every detail in the menacing face only a few feet above his. Its mouth was full of razor-sharp fangs longer than his finger. The eyes were large, almond-shaped black pools of evil and madness. Its grey skin stretched taut over blunted features. Rippling muscles strained in its long neck. He knew that once his back hit the water below, its talons would impale him, and its fangs would close over his face as it landed.

He did the only thing he could. With the elven blade clenched tightly, the boy brought the tip under the creature's heart and clasped the hilt with both hands. The water hit his back with a loud clap and the demon landed on him an instant later. He felt the tip of his sword go deep into its chest until it stopped at the hilt. The force pushed him under the water. Chip almost lost consciousness from the impact and felt the air leave his lungs as the hilt of the sword pushed down on his chest, causing a sharp pain. He felt the creature's fangs surround his face and draw blood, but it stopped moving as they sank, and then the current separated them. Something grabbed his collar and yanked him up. Chip gasped for air and tried to bring his sword around, expecting another demon, but it was Garth Stone.

"Hang on!"

They plunged again over the next step, though this one was half as tall. Chip went through the water and struck the bottom hard. Not giving up, he pushed upwards with his failing strength and broke through the surface. The orphan had time to suck in a breath of fresh air before enduring two more drops that ended in a large, shallow pool. The entire side of the pool fell off into a huge waterfall at the far side.

The people of Vanalon called them the High Falls. Many villagers had fallen in the Rocky River over the years to be carried over this waterfall to their deaths. The strong current took the weary companions towards the edge where they could see the kingdom below in the valley.

The bedraggled companions all frantically paddled to the side of the river to avoid getting swept over. Chip felt exhausted, and his clothes seemed to weigh as much as his body. With fear driving him on, the boy swam with all his remaining strength. It was enough to prevent him from getting closer to the edge, but not enough to make it closer to the bank.

Unluckily, the boy had surfaced on the side of the river with the stronger current compared to the others who came up on the right side. They were able to make it to the bank much easier. Chip's energy began to deplete, and suddenly, the orphan was only a few feet from the edge. A hundred feet below were jagged rocks that would smash his body to pieces. He panicked in fear.

"'Do not give up,'" the weapons master had said to him. It was the one lesson above them all.

The boy thought of how much he wanted to see his best friend and the princess. Memories of his childhood flashed before him. An image of Auntie Clare emerged in his mind, beckoning him forward. He needed to reach her. He wanted to live. The orphan renewed his efforts by kicking with energy he did not know he had. 'When you feel you can't go on, you have lots left.' The saying spurred him on. Incrementally, he went forward a foot closer to the bank, then two. His muscles screamed in protest, but he pushed them even harder. He would not give up. After all, he'd given his word.

Chip gained another foot and then a few more before the current finally lessened and the rest became easier. He reached the edge in a wet heap. Garth pulled him up, and he collapsed on the bank, feeling as if he would never be able to breathe in enough air.

Xander looked miserable but amused as he waited for the boy to recover.

"I could have saved you if necessary with my magic, but it would have alerted the demons to our location," the wizard stated as if discussing the weather. "Besides, I knew you could do it." He smiled at Chip. The boy looked at him in disbelief, still gasping for air.

"You tell me this now?," he panted. Xander laughed and stood up.

They clambered up the bank, bruised and battered. A plop sounded behind them announcing another demon that had managed to survive the ordeal. Garth turned around in a calm manner and waded back a few feet into the river. When the demon swam close to him, he pushed it with the tip of his sword into the main current and watched as the helpless creature flew over the edge into oblivion.

"Demons normally do not like water," the wizard mused as the weapons master reached the bank.

"These were hungry," Garth said. "They needed an energy boost after running all day. You also almost melted their master."

Chip could not help but smile weakly.

"I feel like I hit every rock in the world," the boy groaned. Blood dripped from fang marks on his forehead, but they were not deep.

"You did well," Xander said patting the boy on the shoulder. "I did not expect such strength from Elohan. He was arguably the most proficient Brown Level magic user in the world during his youth. He is a master of earth, wind, and water, like most Browns. Even though he is a Level below Blue, it shows that true mastery must be respected. He has grown stronger. The fact that the Demon King is already sending his Inner Circle through is disquieting, to say the least. Elohan still does not know your true Power, but his suspicions grow. He will report to his Master."

He looked at Chip appraisingly. "I am not sure how you trapped his mind on the bridge, but it worked. I thought you might try to use your Power to push him out, but you showed good restraint. I hope you learned some things from his memories that will assist us in the battle to come. We will talk about this later."

Chip started to ask a question, but Xander raised his hand. "Not now. We must inform the new king of these developments. We will talk tonight, preferably over a glass of mulled wine."

Garth grunted in agreement. They both began walking. The boy shrugged and limped after them.

The afternoon sun had almost disappeared. Its last few rays slanted sideways behind them as they headed east to the valley rim. A few of those rays reached down to touch the tiny kingdom in the distance, but even those winked out as the sun dipped below the Pass of Death. They found a village trail that led to the valley rim and the well-worn path that surrounded it.

Chip stood for a moment on the edge, gazing at his home below. Only a couple of days ago, he had embarked on his Manhood Quest. He shook his head in wonder. In that brief time, his whole world had changed.

The boy had found the adventure he had always wanted, but it wasn't what he had expected. Chip let out a deep sigh and then breathed in the early autumn air.

Change was coming. Nothing would ever be the same again. He knew that behind him was death and destruction, and it was coming for the world of humans. This was likely the last time he would look upon his home as it once was.

Xander and his Protector paused to look at the orphan, and seeing his expression, they turned to face the valley themselves. The three figures stood silhouetted against the darkening sky. All knew the precious little kingdom below was about to be attacked by untold demon hordes.

It was their duty to defend it from this ancient threat.

A boy, a weapons master, and a wizard had pledged their allegiance to do just that. After several moments, they looked at each other, nodded, and started down the path towards the kingdom of Vanalon.

END OF VOLUME ONE.

If you enjoyed reading this, please leave a review on Amazon. It would be greatly appreciated.

Visit my website: www.terryironwood.com

Type your email address at the bottom of the page to be notified of my next book launch.

I have added a free short story prequel called "Weapons Master" in the upper right corner of my website. It is Garth Stone's backstory.

The Orphan's Quest audiobook with special effects is now available on Audible.

Link to Volume Two: Defenders of Hope

I hope you enjoyed Volume 1: Orphan's Quest. Be sure to look out for Volumes 2 to 7 of The Great Forget Fantasy Series!

The Great Forget Fantasy Series:

Volume 1: Orphan's Quest

Volume 2: Defenders of Hope

Volume 3: A Dim World

Volume 4: Guardian

Volume 5: Wizard's Guild

Volume 6: Stone Kingdom

Volume 7: Coming end of December, 2024.

Acknowledgements

I offer my heartfelt thanks to my family and friends, who provided invaluable support, wisdom, and encouragement. You know who you are. I especially want to mention Kevin C., Steve S., and Ward C., who went above and beyond.

I am delighted to work with my editor, Jason Letts from Imbue Editing, who continues to improve my writing.

Last, and certainly not least, I wish to thank an orphan, Chip, for taking me on his quest.

Many thanks,

Terry Ironwood

ABOUT THE AUTHOR

Terry Ironwood resides with his family. He holds multiple university degrees and is interested in the science of self-improvement. He is equally fascinated with physics and spirituality. Terry believes in an 'attitude of gratitude' and is grateful he can write full-time. His dream is to help others reach their full potential.

Printed in Dunstable, United Kingdom